THE EXTINCT

Shigeru Brody

As flies to wanton boys are we to the Gods; they kill us for their sport.

-WILLIAM SHAKESPEARE

1

As soon as the rain stopped and the sun began to shine, they knew something was watching them.

The group of megatherium sat in the shade of trees near what would one day become the La Brea Tar Pits. Weighing more than five tons and more massive than an Indian elephant, megatherium giant sloths were one of the largest land animals that ever lived. They had been feeding all morning on rotting fruit and leaves, glancing behind them at the tall grass. Armed with eighteen-inch claws, they were ready to fight at the first sign of an attack, though there were few predators courageous enough to attempt an assault.

Tucked low in the grass, feline eyes waited patiently for the sloths' apprehensiveness to ease. Smilodon, a fearsome solitary carnivore, licked its foot-long canines. Commonly known as the saber-toothed tiger, smilodon weighed as much as a small car and had the ferocity of a wolverine.

Saliva slopped from the saber-tooth's mouth, its muscles ready to pounce at the first sign of sickness or old age among the megatherium. One of the sloths lay down on its side, dozing off in the hot sun. With a thunderous roar, the cat ripped through the grass, its fourteen hundred pounds accelerating to a speed of thirty miles an hour.

The megatherium froze; this was one of the only predators they refused to fight. They turned and attempted to flee, all except one.

The lone megatherium awoke to the warning calls of the others. It saw the predator closing in, canines spread apart for a killing bite to the throat or midsection. Unable to get away quickly enough, the megatherium stood upright on its hind legs, revealing its full eighteen feet of girth.

Adrenaline coursed through smilodon; megatherium's size and massive claws didn't intimidate him. He ducked his head low as his muscles shivered with anticipation.

The megatherium backed against a tree, urinating on itself out of fear, and waited.

But smilodon was not the only predator that had been hunting them this morning. Bellowing laughter came from the grass. Hyaenodon Gigas, the largest and most vicious mammalian predator the earth has ever seen, sprinted toward its prey. Snout to tail, it was the size of a truck, with jaws that ate every part of a meal, including teeth and bones. With its acute senses, it smelled the urine of the terrified megatherium and the saliva of the smilodon as it raced in for a kill strike.

The megatherium groaned in fear and anguish as the clan of hyaenodon darted for it, only their backs visible in the tall grass. Suddenly, the clan changed course.

The saber-tooth focused on its prey and leapt into the air with its mouth wide open. Its claws dug into the sloth's hide. The sloth writhed in pain and slammed into the ground, the claws on its forelegs useless against the fangs that dug into its neck.

And then, as quickly as the attack had occurred, it stopped. The megatherium was released. It stood, disoriented a few moments, and then dashed for the safety of its numbers.

Smilodon rose from the ground, its vision spinning. It had tasted blood and expected to see the corpse of its prey lying before it. Instead, it saw blood gushing from a deep wound on its hind leg.

Then it saw the movement. In tightening circles, four massive bodies blocked every direction from escape. The smilodon growled and roared, feeling the tug of fear in its belly for the first time in its adult life.

There was the familiar call that sounded like maniacal laughter as the hyaenodon positioned themselves.

One sprinted from behind and bit into smilodon's hindquarters, causing the cat to turn and swipe with its giant paw. As it turned back, a large mass raced for smilodon, the assailant's mouth widening as it aimed for the face. The great beast clamped down into the skull of smilodon, snapping one of the cat's large canines in half. Smilodon was lifted into the air by its head and smashed back into the earth, its skull crushed and its back broken as another beast tore into its belly, biting through organ, muscle, and bone.

There were no other predators to challenge hyaenodon for its kill except for other clans. An apex, adaptable predator, hyaenodon survived cataclysm after cataclysm for millions of years by cunning and ferocity. Hyaenodon lived on nearly every continent and ate everything that could provide nutrition. Believed to be

Shigeru Brody

extinct, hyaenodon would survive, in some of the most remote regions on earth...

2

Dr. Namdi Said sat in the Ministry of Medical Services swatting flies with a plastic swatter. Hyderabad at this time of year was hot and muggy, the air a thick wall of heat making any type of physical exertion laborious.

Namdi sat with his feet up on the desk. The office he'd been given was small and dirty, but there was a window facing out to the busy street. Without stop signs or traffic signals on this block, every few hours the metallic crash of a car accident could be heard.

"Dr. Said," Phillip Reynolds said as he walked in and sat down across from him. He pushed his glasses up onto his forehead and rubbed the bridge of his nose with his thumb and forefinger. "Sorry I'm late. I'm new here. Still haven't figured my way around. I thought Andhra Pradesh was mostly a more civilized part of India, but it's as wild as anywhere else I guess."

"What can I do for you, Mr. Reynolds?"

He pulled out a package of cigarettes and lit one. "Do you mind?"

"Yes, actually."

"Oh," he said, as he took a substantial drag and then put the cigarette out on his shoe, stuffing the butt back into the pack. "I'm here about an American citizen that went missing a couple months back, Davis Larson. His wife's been bugging me damn near every day."

"If you're missing a person you should be talking to the police. There are gangs in the city that kidnap tourists for ransom and—"

"No, it's not a gang," he said, twirling the cigarette package in his hand.

"How do you know?"

"They weren't in the city, they were out in the plains near the Eastern Ghats. I think you should talk to her."

"Mr. Phillips, I'm a doctor for—"

"I know, not your specialty. But I was told you have another specialty in animal attacks."

Namdi stared at him a beat before saying, "Who told you that?"

"Not important."

"It's a hobby. I have no official position or even training, other than treating victims of attacks."

"Understood. But I promised this lady I'd have her talk with an expert and you're the nearest thing to an expert I could find who speaks English. I would consider it a personal favor if you could talk to her. Don't have to do anything, just hear her out."

He slammed his swatter down on the table, smashing a giant fly and causing Reynolds to jump. Namdi smiled at his reaction and said, "Very well, I'll speak with her."

3

Looking down from 12,000 feet over New Hampshire reminded Eric Holden of a jigsaw puzzle. Green and yellow squares with small blips for the buildings and homes. At twenty-two, he'd already completed more than ten jumps, all with his father James who was standing in front of him now, letting him peek over his shoulder at the ground below.

"With the wing-suits we should have a good minute of free-fall," James said. "You ready?"

"Yeah."

James nodded and pulled down his goggles. Eric playfully gave him a push out before James had a chance to jump. He watched his father flip backward and then even out into the traditional spread pose, his wing-suit catching the air and making him appear like some mutant bird slowly drifting down to earth.

Eric gave the pilot a nod and then vaulted from the plane.

The air was icy and stung the unprotected skin on his cheeks like needles. He spread his arms and thighs, allowing the fabric of the wing-suit to stretch and double his drag. He could see Strawberry River from here, winding through lush hillsides like a coiled snake.

Eric pointed his head downward, turning his body vertical, tightened his wing-suit, and shot toward his father. Adrenaline coursed through him, his face turning white and the blood rushing to his organs and away from his extremities. The wind was screaming in his ears and crawling down his neck, freezing his chest and making him shiver. He raced toward his father, who didn't notice him. Upon passing, Eric grabbed the ripcord and pulled his father's chute.

The parachute expanded, causing a surprised James Holden to curse and instinctively reach for the cord to his emergency chute. Eric gave him a thumbs-up from below as his father slowed and began a gentle descent.

Landing on soft grass, Eric unbuckled from the chute and waited for his father to descend. James landed fifteen feet away and unbuckled, a grin across his face as he shook his head.

"That's dangerous."

"You did it first, old man. My first jump. Scared the crap outta me."

Some aides began gathering up the chutes, and James collapsed next to Eric who had laid down on the grass. The sun warmed their faces and a light breeze was blowing cotton strands through the air.

"You still dating that porn star?" James asked.

"She's not a porn star, Dad. She was in a swimsuit ad."

James chuckled. "What was her name?"

"Wendy."

"How's ol' Wendy?"

"Okay, I guess."

"You gotta settle down sometime, Eric. Man needs a family."

He shook his head. "Not for me, thanks. I like bouncing around. I can't picture myself like, holding hands and making dinner and all that. Some people just aren't meant for it, I think. You with anyone?"

"Nah, here and there. Nothing serious. I travel too much. But I wanted to ask you something: I'm going to India for a few weeks. Want to come with?"

"When?"

"A week from today. Hunting elephant."

Eric laughed. "What the hell do you know about hunting elephants?"

"Nothing. That's why I've hired a guide. An old friend of me and your mother's. It's not exactly legal over there. You in?"

"I don't kill animals, Pops. I skipped school the other day because a cat was stuck in the alley behind my apartment and I spent all day coaxing him out and getting him fed and cleaned up. I sure as shit am not shooting something as beautiful as an elephant."

"That's life buddy boy. We all live and die, part of the cycle. But don't worry about it. Next time then."

4

From *Visiting Andhra Pradesh: A Manual for First-Time Tourists:*

Though Andhra Pradesh is only India's fifth-largest state by population, it has the longest coastline in the country along the Bay of Bengal and dense jungles filled with insect species and plant life that has yet to be cataloged. Farther from the coast, the jungle recedes into the vast open plains of the Deccan Plateau that stretch for hundreds of miles. Rolling green hills and jagged mountains are split open from mighty rivers, and the climate, though bearable, makes many middle class and wealthier Indians likely to find their homes in the densely populated cities rather than the smaller, agrarian villages dotting the countryside.

The café in downtown Hyderabad, Andhra Pradesh's capital city, was crowded with tourists. Many were from Europe and even more from the Middle East, who found the proximity and low cost of a trip to Andhra Pradesh appealing.

Dr. Said sat at a table in the corner, sipping Turkish

coffee. Some businessmen were seated at the booth next to him, telling jokes about women. Namdi would bet they were cowards at home, bending to the will of wives they feared.

A tall blonde walked into the café and asked a waiter something. The waiter pointed to Namdi, and the woman came over. Her eyes were rimmed red, and she wore no make-up, her hair pulled back and held in place with a rubber-band.

"Dr. Said?" she said.

"Yes."

She held out her hand. It was soft and lotioned. "Nancy Larson."

"Nice to meet you. Sit down, please."

She sat down and placed her purse on the table. Namdi noticed there was a box of tissues inside and, tucked away underneath, a small handgun.

"What can I do for you, Mrs. Larson?"

"Phillip told me you were an expert on the animals in Andhra Pradesh. That you help governments catch animals that start attacking people."

"I have in the past, yes."

She pulled out a photo and slid it across the table. It was her and a thin, white male in shorts and a tank-top standing next to a jeep.

"This is my husband, Davis. He went missing thirty-six days ago."

"Where?"

"We were near the coast. I was driving that jeep in the picture. We had come for a picture safari. Davis used to love hunting, but I got him off that. I told him it was cruel and that taking a good picture was just as hard as taking a good shot. I don't think he ever believed me, but he did it anyway." Nancy took out a tissue from her purse and held it in her hands, twirling the thin paper over and over again. "We saw . . . something. It was fur that went along some bushes next to the jeep. Davis wanted a photo so we stopped. He thought it might be a wildebeest or something.

"We were speaking about the World Cup that was coming up soon and he was waiting for his photo. I turned to get some water. I just looked away for a second. When I turned back . . . he was gone. No sounds. He was just gone. I yelled for him and ran around looking for him, even though the hairs on my neck were standing up. I felt like that was an evil place. I still do. But I saw these next to the jeep."

Nancy pulled out more photos. Namdi took them and held them up. They were prints in the soft dirt. Paws. In one photo, Nancy put her hand next to the paw print. Smart girl, he thought. Without perspective, no one would've believed it.

"These prints—" Namdi began.

"Are huge. I know. I've shown them to other people too. They said they had to be a hoax."

"Are these the only photos you have?"

"No, I have a few more. But I was only there five or ten minutes before I sped to the police station. We searched for three days. We didn't even find a shred of clothing. It's like the earth swallowed him."

He put the photos down. "Mrs. Larson, I'm going to be honest with you because I do not want to give you false hope. There is little chance that he could survive for more than a month on the plains without food or water. Have you considered that maybe he ran away and planned this?"

"Ran away? He didn't run away. We had a good marriage. And if he wanted to leave, he had better opportunities than that."

Namdi glanced at the businessmen next to them as they rose to leave, taking a few glances at Nancy as they did so. "What is it you'd like me to do?"

"Find out what happened to him. It's the not knowing that's killing me. I just need to know what happened. Could a rogue tiger or something have done this?"

"Possibly. When an animal sees how easy prey human beings are, it will only hunt human beings. These are very dangerous animals. The only way to stop them is to kill them. But I've never heard of a case like this. Where nothing is found. It may have been bandits or militia, and the prints are distortions due to the weather."

"Will you help me?"

Namdi saw tears in her eyes and watched as she tore the tissue to shreds in her hands, the pieces flaking down across her lap and onto the floor. He remembered a similar reaction in his mother when the army had informed them that his father would not be coming home.

"All right, Mrs. Larson. I will look into it."

As the sun set and baked the sky a soft pink, Namdi Said sat at his desk and reviewed all the photos Mrs. Nancy Larson had taken the day her husband went missing. The paw prints were the most interesting of course, but there was something else. On the side of the passenger seat, indented into the fabric, were punctures arched in a semi-circle. There was little fabric torn away. Namdi thought that whatever punctured them would have to be as sharp as razors to not tear anything apart.

He pressed a button on his phone. "Ms. Bai?"

"Yes, doctor?"

"Call the police and the Department of Wildlife, please. Get me the files for every missing person and potential animal attack on the plains for the last six months. Start with around Hyderabad and work your way out. Nothing in the cities, just the plains."

"Yes, sir. It may take me some time."

"That is fine. Thank you."

Namdi threw the photos down and leaned back in his seat. He didn't like this case. If Nancy was telling an accurate account, her husband had been taken in total silence in broad daylight with another person nearby. Tigers and panthers had killed and kidnapped before, but never so brazenly. Something was different.

He noticed for the first time that the hair on his neck was standing up.

5

Blood coated Thomas' hands.

He sat near the fire, watching the flames flicker in the darkness, sipping whiskey from a flask kept in his breast pocket. This far inland from the coast Andhra Pradesh had no light pollution. The sky was blanketed in the sparkle of stars, the moon a bright slit in the blackness over lush plains.

Thomas glanced at the other men around the fire, their faces worn and tired, small droplets of black darkening their clothes as if it had rained blood. Robert Mason. Not a hunter. Scared and maybe a little dangerous because of his fear. James Holden sat poking a stick into the fire, watching the crimson embers dance in flames.

The hunt had gone well. They'd followed a herd of Asian elephants for more than three days before the bull separated himself from the rest and they could begin taking shots. The Andhra Pradeshn Park Authorities kept close tabs on all hunters, especially those with British and American passports. Not unwarranted considering the history of colonialism and abuse suffered at the hands of the crown. Rape and genocide and slavery. The people here had no trust for white men, even those that paid handsomely.

If they had killed a cow, or worse, a calf, they would have had to spend the rest of their funds bribing their way out of a prison sentence.

Mason spat in the fire and said, "I'm going to miss these nights. The grass has a sweet smell to it here I haven't found anywhere else."

"Like cow shit with sugar on it," James Holden said. He looked out over a herd of Sambar deer, a dark roving mass in the pale light of the moon. "Good hunt, though. Thought Thomas'd drop the rifle and run when that bull charged."

"That's the best time to shoot," Thomas said. "Granted they're more impervious to pain, but they face you squarely, and you can have an excellent target if you know what to look for. Asian elephants here hold their necks at a forty-five-degree angle, so it makes it harder. But an African elephant keeps it horizontal so when they charge, you have a direct shot into the brain. I remember —"

A noise echoed through the night. It seemed to come from the east, and they turned toward it. There was nothing they could see except tall grass and weeds.

Thomas was the expert of the group but also happened to be the drunkest right now and didn't feel like chasing sounds in the dark. "There are tigers," Thomas said, a hint of pleasure in his voice as he saw the looks of his companions. "I wouldn't worry though; I've led tours through this region for twenty years, and they haven't killed a tourist in, oh ... a good ten."

More noises in the dark, closer this time. They seemingly came from the darkness itself as there was little else to hide behind.

"Sounds like laughing," James said.

"There's no people here," Thomas said, putting down his flask and gulping coffee out of a tin cup before picking up his rifle. He slung it over his shoulder and walked toward the noise, leaving his boots behind and opting to go barefoot.

The dirt and grass were warm under his feet, the fire a warm glow in the distance behind him. Their kill lay like a boulder up ahead, the blood congealed in thick gelatin around the carcass. Thomas kneeled and checked the rifle; it was chambered. He held it up in front of him, the shoulder rest tucked firmly against the crook between his chest and arm.

Except for the symphony of crickets that increased in volume as he came away from the fire, there was little noise. No laughing, only hooves in the distance. Thomas strained to hear, exploring with his eyes like they could pick up subtle sounds that his ears could not. As if his hearing needed to adjust to the darkness as much as his sight, he began to hear something. Slow, rhythmic breathing. Deep; a pant.

It was an animal.

From the depth of the breathing, he guessed it was immense. He brought his rifle up to firing position and looked down the sight, the barrel firmly aimed at the breathing. *Coming from the carcass? Maybe the bull isn't dead?*

But the moonlight illuminated the body enough that he could see the great belly of the elephant which would have been rising and falling if it were alive.

There was light behind the carcass — yellow orbs reflecting the moon with confident fierceness. The figure behind the spheres began to take shape: thick head, robust body, and short legs. A tigress.

She was growling, preparing to defend her scavenged meal. Thomas took aim, the barrel pointed squarely at her face, waiting for her to lunge. He needed to wait until she moved; she might retreat. It'd be better if she fled.

The beast turned its head west, toward the camp. Thomas could see the muscles bulge underneath her fur, even with the moon as his only light. The tigress let out a soft whine and then turned away from the carcass, building to a slow gallop, disappearing into the night.

Thomas exhaled; he hadn't realized he'd been holding his breath, but now his lungs ached. Would he have been able to hit his target, a moving target, at night? He stood and wiped at the dirt on his knee. His fingers tingled as blood returned to them, a wave of calm washing over him as he looked up to the moon as if the light could warm his face like sunshine.

A roar.

Bassed so heavily Thomas felt it in his feet, rising from the ground, like the plains themselves had roared. The sound came from all directions. It filled the air and echoed across the valley.

As he tried to rein in his thoughts, he realized there were other sounds. They were screams.

Thomas sprinted through the grass toward the fire, the sounds of screams echoing in his head. Then silence. He stopped, panting, heart pounding in his ears as adrenaline coursed through him like fire. He started running again until he was near the camp and saw there was no one there: a spilled flask of whiskey lying in the dirt, blood spattered across it. Their tents were torn to shreds, supplies smashed into the ground. Logs had been knocked out of the fire, and the smoldering wood was cooling in the night air.

Thomas crept past the fire, not breeching the limit of illumination less than a few meters away. He couldn't see anything aside from the tall grass though his senses were more attuned from fear. The fire was dying. He took a few paces back to stand next to it, listening to his own breath as sweat rolled down his forehead.

There were eyes in the darkness. Not the circular yellow of the tigress, pinpoints of red. Small flames hanging above the ground. The eyes were affixed on him and he couldn't move. His muscles were heavy and tight, and he made a conscious effort to relax them.

Another roar ripped through the night, followed by what sounded like laughter. He could hear the deep pant of the beast's breathing and the slow thumping of an immense heart. He took a few paces back, and the red eyes grew tighter, small slits nearly invisible in the night accompanied by a growl.

Thomas knew he had two options: shoot or run. He was too close to get off more than one shot. One shot in the dark at a quick-moving animal. He thought about standing still; not giving ground sometimes worked with the big cats. Although predators could smell the sweat of fear and hear the increased beating of their prey's heart, nothing triggered their savage instincts more than fleeing prey. They were meant to chase.

His mind was blank, with no thoughts able to penetrate the cloud of anxiety and fear. A bare instinct of survival bubbled up in his gut, and he ran.

The wind was against his face as he focused on keeping his balance on the uneven ground. The periphery of his vision blurred until he could only see what was in front him, a vague impression that he didn't have a clear run ahead. He didn't need to look behind him; he felt the enormous animal's paws hitting the ground, the sound of heavy breathing closing in on him. Thomas sprinted for the elephant carcass as he felt hot breath against the skin of his neck. He bounded over the bull's carcass, hoping to lure the predator to the stink of meat and blood and away from him. His foot caught on the rough hide and then a white flash, his jaw absorbing most of the impact as he hit the ground.

Dazed and on his back, the blood seeped out of his mouth. The animal behind him slowed.

A shot crackled through the air, and Thomas looked toward the fire. James stood there with a rifle in one arm, his clothes torn and stained black. His other arm was nearly severed at the shoulder, pouring blood into the dry earth. He tossed the rifle to the ground and pulled a .45 caliber Smith & Wesson handgun from his waist.

The animal turned and ran for him. As Thomas lost consciousness, the last sounds that reached his ears were gunshots and screams, and the wet sounds of an animal feeding.

6

The University of New Hampshire campus was beautiful during the summer months, numerous trees and shrubbery showing off lush greens and yellows. Eric typically spent the summers with his father in Manhattan and enjoyed the pure energy that a large city could exude, but he always missed the crystal blue skies and trees of campus.

He'd be leaving for New York in two weeks and was looking forward to time with his father. Though his parents had divorced soon after they had him, he and his father had always stayed close, spending long summers traveling to exotic locations Eric hadn't heard of, like Belmopan or Santa Rosa. His father loved to travel. Said it kept the soul awake. There was some truth in it, Eric guessed. But almost twenty now, he knew that that wasn't the sole reason his father was always gone. Too much travel could turn one into a stranger at home, which was exactly what his father wanted.

They didn't talk much about his father's job as an investment banker, but it was understood that it was miserable. A lot of hours in exchange for a lot of money. The type of situation where one needs to trade joy for a fat paycheck. Where it seemed Eric was headed, and he didn't know how to change his trajectory.

A black sedan pulled into the parking lot and circled around until it came to where Eric was seated and waiting for his mother to pick him up for lunch. He stood and wiped at the dirt that had clung to his shorts and walked to the passenger door. He hesitated when he saw that his mother wasn't driving; it was his step-father, Jeff.

"What're you doing here?" Eric said as he climbed in and sat down.

"Your mom couldn't drive today, kid. She's pretty screwed up right now, so I want you to take it easy on her."

"What'dya mean screwed up? What happened?"

Jeff glanced out the window at a group of passing girls and then pulled away from the curb. "Your father's dead, Eric."

Eric's heart felt like it slumped in his chest; his stomach churned, butterflies tingling his belly and causing nausea. He thought he would vomit.

"He died in India, kid. He was there on some safari or some shit."

Eric's throat clenched, and tears welled up in his eyes, but he fought them back and looked out the window, his reflection absently looking back at him. "How do you know? I mean, things can get reported wron—"

"They're bringing back his body tomorrow for burial. What's left of it anyway."

Eric looked over at his step-father; his face was stern, but there was a glimmer of pleasure in his eyes. Jeff had always felt inadequate compared to his father. Whenever they'd get in a fight, Eric's mother would say she wished she'd never gotten divorced from James. It would cut deep since Jeff knew it was true.

"How'd he die?" Eric said.

"You don't want to know."

"How, Jeff?"

Jeff looked at him and then back out at the road. "He was killed by an animal."

"What animal?"

"I don't know. A tiger or somethin'."

They got on the freeway and were silent for a long time.

"Look," Jeff said, "he lived a crazy life your father. This type of thing was inevitable. The important thing now is that you take care of your mom. For whatever reason, she's taking it pretty hard. And if she's takin' it hard, it means she's gonna annoy the shit outta me."

Eric felt the urge to reach over and slap Jeff, but instead he kept staring out the window, watching the passing strip malls and fast-food restaurants and pool halls as they approached his mother's house.

It was a cold thing to say, and Jeff had said it out of spite, but there was some truth to it. His father had lived like a man who wanted to die, though he always said he was afraid of it.

They parked on the street in front of the house and Eric got out, choosing to walk across the lawn rather than share the sidewalk with Jeff. The grass was thick and shaggy from months of not being cut, patches of yellow beginning to pop up everywhere. Eric opened the front door; the inside of the house was much cleaner than the outside, carpets freshly washed and furniture dusted, the smell of lemon polish hanging in the air.

His mother was lying on the couch, the TV turned low. Eric sat down by her feet without saying a word, and she pulled her legs up to make room, not taking her eyes off the television.

"I'll be out in the garage," Jeff said.

Eric watched Jeff walk out. He remembered when his father had built that garage. All in one summer. Eric was eight at the time and he remembered the smell of sawdust and the taste of lemonade as he helped his father, carrying tools and hammering nails. James had even let him use a nail gun a couple times, but the sound had scared him and his father put it away, even though it increased the amount of work he needed to do.

"How you doing, Mom?" She didn't say anything. "Are they sure?" Eric said hopefully. "I mean, mistakes happen. It could be someone else, right?"

His mother watched television as if she hadn't heard him. She took a moment and then turned to him, her eyes red and puffy. "He was a good man, Eric. I don't want you to ever be mad at him for going on those trips. They kept him alive."

"I know," he said. From this close, he could smell the sweet aroma of peach Schnapps emanating from her. "This is the way he would've wanted to go, I guess," he said in a clumsy attempt to comfort her.

"I don't think I ever stopped loving him," she said, turning back to the television. "I hated him too, though. I loved him and hated him. He could make me feel like the most important person in the world one day and a piece of shit the next. But I still loved him, I never stopped."

Eric rubbed her calf; it was soft, fragile. "I know, Mom. He loved you too." Eric could see the dining table from where he was sitting, and an old photo of his father in a Navy uniform was out, a box with his medals open next to it. "How did you find out?"

"His sister called me."

"Kathy?"

His mother nodded.

"Where is she now?"

"Borneo I think. She's married to some spiritual guru. That whole family's screwed up."

Eric sat with his mother a few more minutes and then gave her a kiss on the cheek before going to his bedroom.

His old room had been kept the same as when he had moved out, even though Jeff wanted to put a pool table and a bar in.

Eric collapsed on his bed and stared at the ceiling, waves of emotion going through him before he felt the soft flow of tears on his cheeks.

7

Eric woke to the claustrophobic tightness of a dark room. It took some time for his eyes to adjust and he stared out the window at the sky, the moon covered with slow-moving gray clouds.

The alarm clock said 7:27 pm, and he rose and walked out of the room. His mother was still lying on the couch, an empty bottle of Schnapps on the coffee table in front of her. Eric tip-toed out of the house and slowly shut the door behind him before making his way to the sidewalk, looking back to the house one more time before moving on.

The night air was cool, the smell of fern and mountain air fresh in his nostrils. His cell phone had three messages, but he turned it off without listening. After a few minutes of walking, he stopped at the nearest bus stop and sat on the bench, watching the cars drive by like white-eyed demons through the night. They appeared sinister. It was funny how the most innocuous things could appear wicked when you had wickedness done to you.

There was a convenience store across the street, and the clerk was eating a burrito and watching a small television behind the counter, not paying attention to the two older men that were shoving donuts into their jackets. Eventually the men bought a fountain drink and the clerk didn't think it odd that two men had roamed the store for ten minutes to buy only one drink.

The bus approached, its engine thundering down the street until coming to a stop a little past Eric. He climbed on and nodded to the driver before taking the first seat. An old woman sat at the back of the bus staring out the window. It didn't look like she was focused on anything in particular. A wrinkled and worn face, lit by the passing lights of street lamps before dimming.

He thought about his first night at the dorms, and how quickly his father had picked up the mother of a girl down the hall. James had always been in love with one woman or another, falling hard one week and growing bored the next. It was the reason his parents got divorced. In a way, Eric understood it. People had just one life and wanted to enjoy it to the fullest. But James wasn't around to hear his wife crying herself to sleep every night; Eric was. Still, his father had always told him family first, though he didn't seem to practice what he preached.

Eric sighed as the bus got near the dorms and he was let off. The funeral would be in a few days, and it was going to be the last time he would get to see his father.

8

From *Visiting Andhra Pradesh: A Manual for First-Time Tourists:*

Andhra Pradesh has often been a top destination for thrill-seekers and tourists. With its diverse landscapes, masses of animals found in few other places, and breathtaking sunsets, some have found it a prime vacation spot despite it being in a second world country with the usual problems of any significant swath of any nation, namely crime, and poverty.

Near the city of Kavali is a string of houses owned by wealthy investors—usually European and American real estate moguls or investment firms—leased to vacationers for periods of one week to one month. The houses are far apart from one another, enough so that vacationers can enjoy their privacy but still have others nearby should they require something. Many tourists find these homes comfortable and safe and yet still close enough to major natural tourist sites to be appealing. Please check with your travel guide for availability dates.

A family stepped onto the porch of one of the homes. The two boys ran into a nearby patch of forest, yelling and laughing. Their mother was a slim woman in a white dress, straw hat pulled down to cover her eyes from the scorching sun. Her husband wrapped his arms around her waist and gave her a kiss on the neck as they watched the boys run around.

"I can't believe we actually found someplace they like," the man said.

"I like it too," she said. "The locals are a hassle, though."

"They're all right, just trying to make a buck like anyone else."

"Are you kidding? You can't even get lunch without being attacked with that cheap garbage they're trying to sell."

The man shrugged. "What you feel like doing?"

"Let's go into town and have a drink. I hear all the street merchants have to leave before night."

"What about the kids?"

"No one's gonna care if they're with us."

The man kissed her neck again and nibbled on her ear, causing her to giggle and pull away.

"I've got to shower and change," the man said, opening the front door.

"Don't take too long."

The woman sat down on a wooden bench and looked out over the vast expanse before her. There was a large patch of grass in front of the house with a path through it that led to the road back to Kavali on one side and into the dense forest on the other. A tree was near the house, huge with twisted, leafless branches. This was a pretty place she decided, but just too damn hot and humid.

It suddenly became apparent to her that she couldn't hear the boys anymore. Scanning the grass, she couldn't see any movement. "Friedrich," she yelled. "Steven, don't go far. You hear me, boys?"

She stood up and walked off the porch onto the soft dirt. "Friedrich, Steven." There was no reply. Just the hushed whispers of the breeze flowing through the grass. She could hear birds up in the tree and there was the distant hum of a passing plane overhead. The woman hiked into the grass, worry causing her heart to drop. "Boys, if this is a joke, you're grounded, you hear me?"

Worry turned to panic, and she began running through the grass and into the canopy of the forest. The shrubbery and trees grew tightly packed and the sunlight was blocked by foliage. "Friedrich! Steven!" she yelled. The vegetation was thick and inflexible. It made the skin on her arms itch.

There was noise nearby, as if the shrubbery had been spread apart quickly. A shiver went down her back and the hairs on her neck stood straight, but she wasn't sure why.

There was laughter just to the right of her. She turned toward it. "Boys!"

As she took a step forward, she felt a tremendous tug on her arm that threw her forward to the ground. She screamed as she hit the dirt, confusion and fear taking hold. She went to pick herself up and realized she couldn't.

Her arm had been severed at the bicep and blood cascaded down from the ragged flesh, coloring her white dress a dark red. "No!" she screamed. "Someone help me!

Help me! Hel—"

Another tug and the world spun and turned black. The screams stopped, and the hushed breeze blew again.

The husband came out of the house a while later and flipped on a pair of sunglasses. It was going to be hot even at night, so he'd only worn shorts and a cotton button-up. The breeze felt nice against his bare legs, and he stood on the porch and enjoyed it.

The sun was so bright he had to squint even with sunglasses.

He stepped off the porch and walked along the path through the grass to the rented jeep he was convinced he'd been overcharged on. His family wasn't inside. He turned back toward the grass and looked around. "Katherine?" he yelled out. "Boys?" He walked back the way he came and went inside the house. The living room was empty. The kitchen was empty and so were the basement and the upstairs bedroom. They must've gone for a walk or something.

The man flopped on the couch in the living room and decided he would wait for them. He walked outside every few minutes and looked around, but no one came. Finally he decided he would drive around and look for them.

As he stepped out of the house, he froze. Vultures were flying down into the forest canopy, their bald heads held stiffly between their slim shoulders as they drifted toward the ground. They were far larger than he thought they would be. He wondered what they would be doing here, then his eyes widened and his heart skipped a beat. "Katherine!"

He ran into the jungle as the vultures scattered into the air. One was on the ground near him and he kicked at it and it bit him on the shin before flapping its wings and flying off over the grass. They didn't leave the kill, just waited nearby; they had grown patient over time and could wait for days.

The man dropped to his knees when he saw what they had been feeding on: a mass of bone and sinew with bits of ragged flesh attached, a white dress torn to pieces on the dirt. Vomit burst out of the man's mouth, and he stumbled back.

He sat weeping on the ground as the vultures, slowly and quietly, began their descent back to the kill.

9

The funeral parlor had a splash of taste in the décor but little in the owners. They had bought the funeral home as an investment only a few years ago, and it was turning out to be more work than profit. They seemed to dislike the dead and hated grieving relatives even more. More than one family had to tell the receptionist to quit talking on the phone during a service or say to a mortician to turn down the television or tell the director not to let her children run around.

Eric sat in the front row next to his mother and Jeff. Jeff had chosen this place because he said his mother's service had been here, but Eric knew it was to save money. James' estate would be divided soon and Eric and his mom would be receiving a sizeable share. Jeff had no intention of letting his wife spend it on frivolous expenses like her ex-husband's funeral.

Eric had dreamed last night of his father. He'd seen his broken body in some ditch in India, covered with flies and maggots, his entrails spilled out onto his lap. India appeared like a graveyard in his dreams. The sky was red and gray. The rivers were dirty and all the animals were decomposing, their slick flesh exposed underneath open sores. The dream came more than once and woke him up each time, cold sweat making his shirt cling to him.

But his fear from last night had transformed into annoyance today. He felt agitated, not wanting to be around anyone or do anything. Irritation wasn't an emotion he frequently felt and he didn't know the mechanisms to deal with it effectively. It just sat in the pit of his stomach like jagged metal, weighing him down and clouding his thoughts.

Some of the mourners would genuinely miss his father. A few friends and co-workers and girlfriends. One of his girlfriends, a blonde named Brittney, knelt in front of him.

"How are ya, darlin'?" she said in her Southern drawl.

"I'm holding up. How've you been?"

"Not so good since your daddy left us. I'm gonna miss him, you know. He always had a way a cheerin' me up." She looked over at Eric's mother, giving her an icy stare, and decided to cut the conversation short. "I just wanted to tell ya that if ya needed anythin', don't hesitate to give me a ring. Okay?"

"Thanks."

She smiled and squeezed his hand before returning to her seat.

Brittney really would miss his father. But most of the people there only showed up because they thought it would look inappropriate if they didn't. The way they were laughing and talking—trying to keep their voices to a whisper but never succeeding—it looked like they'd forgotten him already.

Though she'd been emotional yesterday, his mother seemed fine today. Eric wondered if she'd taken something.

His mother stood and began walking around the room, chatting with the guests. Before long she was mingling and men were flirting with her while Jeff stewed in his seat and watched her from behind sunglasses.

Eric searched the room, looking for familiar faces. There was one face that didn't look familiar at all. It was old and tan, leathery almost; like it'd had too much exposure to sun and wind. The man sat quietly in the back, not speaking with anyone.

The man saw him staring and grinned. Eric turned around, facing the casket again; the service was starting.

It was customary to wait a day between a viewing and the funeral, but the director of the parlor had urged that they take place the same day and Jeff agreed. There was no doubt in Eric's mind that some sort of deal had been worked out.

After the service, the body was carried out to a hearse and Eric was one of the pallbearers. He drove behind the vehicle with his mother and Jeff, aggravated that Jeff was listening to the radio and humming along with the melody of some old rock song.

The wind was blowing, and leaves were all over the cemetery, rattling softly in the background as a priest stood to deliver a sermon that he had memorized and repeated to the point where he spoke it with neither passion nor conviction.

Eric laid a flower on the casket which had stayed closed the whole time. He wouldn't get to see his father again to say goodbye. As he was walking with his mother back to the car, he noticed the man from the funeral home again. The man stood by the grave until the dirt piled high on top of it and then said something and turned away toward the parking lot.

"I'll meet you at the car, Mom," Eric said. He went back toward the man. "Hi," he said.

"Hello," the man said.

"Were you a friend of my father's?"

The man's lips parted in a smile. "You're Eric, ah? Your dad talked a lot about you." He thrust out his hand. "Thomas Keets."

Eric shook it. "Eric Holden."

"I was with your father when he died. He talked about you quite a lot. He was proud of the man you'd become."

Eric watched him a moment. "How long did you know him for?"

"Well, me and your father went back a long time." Thomas looked to the grave once more and took out a pair of sunglasses, flipping them on and turning back to Eric. "I'd like to talk to you before I go. Let's go get a drink somewhere."

"Um, sure," Eric said. "There's a bar south of the university campus called McPaul's. I can come by around four."

"That's fine," Thomas said. "I'll see you then."

Eric watched him leave. Thomas walked without any pretense; like he didn't realize or care that others could be watching him. He didn't look back and didn't say goodbye to anybody.

Eric faced his father's grave. Tomorrow, it would just be a slab of marble sticking out of the ground, and the memory of his father would slowly start to fade away.

Bye, Pop.

10

The bar was dirty and cluttered with posters, sports memorabilia and neon signs. It stunk of spills that hadn't been cleaned. It wasn't crowded; the night had just begun, but with few other bars nearby, it would be filled with people in less than a couple hours.

Eric sat at the bar, sipping a beer and smoking clove cigarettes.

Thomas walked in and stood by the door, scanning faces in booths and tables before spotting Eric. He sat down next to him and ordered a scotch and water. "May I have one of those?" he said, motioning to the package of clove cigarettes. Eric gave him one and lit it with a lighter. Thomas took a long pull, letting the smoke whirl around him before he spoke. "Do you know how your father died?"

"An animal attack. My stepdad said maybe it was a tiger."

"It wasn't a tiger."

"What was it?"

He took a drag off the cigarette and stared at the small pinpoint of red on the tip. "Doesn't matter. What matters is he died saving my life."

"That doesn't make me feel much better."

Thomas nodded. "I'm a guide," he said, as if he hadn't heard him. "Primarily just Andhra Pradesh but occasionally I'll go farther out if there's work, a wealthy client or whatnot. I had your father and one of his friends with me then. They wanted to hunt bull elephants for a while, which is illegal, but a special license can be granted if you have the money. I suppose there are licenses for any manner of things if you have the money." He stopped and took a drink; chasing it with water. "You know, tribes in Kenya think the big predators are spirits of their ancestors, there to protect the land from invaders."

"And you believe that?"

"No. But I suppose anything's possible." Thomas finished off his scotch and ordered another. He drank what remained of the water.

"Did you see what killed my father?"

He nodded. "I did."

"What was it?"

"I'm not sure."

Thomas took out a pipe and loaded it from a small silk pouch. He took a few puffs and then handed it to Eric. "It's *tobash caruit* from Herat. An exceptional kind of tobacco."

Eric took a puff and felt the smoke going down into his lungs, silky with almost a cherry flavor. "It's good."

Thomas nodded as he took the pipe back. They sat in silence a while, enjoying the smell of the smoke mingling with that of the beer.

"You know, I knew your mother before I knew your father," Thomas said.

"He mentioned that. How did you know her?"

"We were lovers once upon a time. Before she met your father."

"Well that's disgusting."

He grinned and handed the pipe back to Eric. "I was always away on my hunts; it's no life for marriage. Your mother and I parted ways and she met your father. When I came back to the States after a particularly long tour and wanted her back, she was already married. But she did introduce me to your father and we became friends. One of my most loyal clients as well." Thomas put a little more tobacco into the pipe. "The animal that killed your father is becoming quite the legend."

"What do you mean?"

"It's killed at least thirty others, mostly children from the more remote villages who wander off. I'm going to kill it. I want you to come with me."

Eric was silent a moment and then chuckled. "Yeah, right."

"I'm serious."

"Thanks, but no. I'll pass."

"Don't be so hasty. You should consider it."

"Why would I possibly want to fly halfway around the world with you to kill an animal?"

"Because, boy, sometimes a man needs vengeance. If your father died of malaria or a fever, you wouldn't be able to get closure from vengeance, but he didn't. He died from an animal, one that is killing others. I'm offering you the opportunity to get the closure you will need to move on. You're young now and don't realize it, but men need vengeance. It calms the soul. I'm offering this to you because I know that James would offer it to my own son were our roles reversed. We were warriors, he and I, and warriors don't let the deaths of their tribe go unavenged."

He took a pull off the pipe.

"I lost my father when I was young, too. He was a captain in the navy and died in Vietnam. When I was old enough, I moved there... and, anyway, it helped. *Sometimes*, boy, vengeance can bring peace. Especially a righteous vengeance."

Eric drank down the last of his beer. "Gotta piss."

He went to the bathroom, which was surprisingly clean, and urinated. After he washed his hands, he stared at himself in the mirror. He had forgotten how much he looked like his father.

Was what Thomas said true? Could vengeance bring you peace? Because right now it felt as if his insides were torn up. His father had been his best friend and mentor, and Eric knew the full effect of losing him hadn't hit yet. When it did, he was worried it would spiral him. He was prone to depression—the last one having lasted nearly six months when he was seventeen.

"You all right?" someone standing at the urinal said.

"Fine, man. Just thinking."

"Shit, don't do too much'a that."

Eric sighed. "You ever been to India?"

"What?"

He shook his head. "Nothing."

He took a deep breath and went back to Thomas.

11

Dr. Namdi Said had lived in Andhra Pradesh briefly as a child though he was originally from Somalia. He remembered only the droves of merchants lined up on the streets of Kavali, yelling and haggling with any tourist that wandered by, a sight that, though still in existence, had died down with modern conveniences like the internet. He had not seen the plains—named by the locals, "Gold Mines of India," because of the color of the landscape given by the tall yellow grass—until he was in his late twenties and out of medical school.

The jeep he drove in was well past its prime, rust adorning the underside and a constant clicking sound accompanying every rotation of the front wheels. The road to Saint Anthony's Medical Outpost was bumpy and littered with old bones from animals that had leapt in front of moving vehicles. It was rough terrain. More than one person died every week in the plains from animal attacks, from getting lost, disease... there were thousands of deaths awaiting them here.

The medical outpost had been established by a United Nations relief effort to help the outlying villages attain medical care. It was little more than a couple of operating rooms and a limited pharmacy, but it was better than nothing. In years past the various bureaucrats had sapped the villages of whatever value they possessed. Sometimes it was just taking livestock and precious metals. It was rumored by the locals that other times it was pushing the villagers into forced labor. If the bureaucrats and crime bosses here couldn't use them, they would be rented to other nations. These were people in the lowest caste of society; even their own government saw them as little more than animals, though the thought of the local government selling slaves to other nations was too much to believe.

But Namdi had seen such brutality in the diamond mines of the Congo in his work with Doctors Without Borders. An entire village in the Congo was ransacked. The girls and women were forced into prostitution, chained up on a military base. The boys and men were taken to the jungles, a mine called *N'su havu*.

He remembered the stink of the mines more than anything else. Since work was never allowed to stop, the laborers would have to urinate and defecate on themselves. They slept in a nearby cave and were given the barest minimum sustenance to survive, usually some type of gruel made from animal entrails and whatever else happened to be in the vicinity of the mines. They were given only a few cups of water. In the soaring heat and humidity, it was not enough to stave off severe dehydration. Most of the laborers died because of the lack of water. They would fall in the mines and their bodies would remain there the rest of the day.

When the day ended, the other workers would haul the bodies to the surface and throw them in a ditch or leave them out in the jungle. It was rumored that the Congolese government recycled the corpses as meat, claiming it to be beef, mixing it with real beef to sell in foreign markets. Namdi hadn't personally seen it, but he had no doubt it could be true. Once dehumanization occurred, anyone was capable of anything.

The medical outpost was about a hundred yards off the side of the road, made of gray cement with a black roof. There was a policeman's car out front and a tall Bengalis man in a green uniform sat on the hood smoking a cigarette. He put the cigarette out and hopped off the car when he saw Namdi's jeep pull in and park.

"Dr. Said?" the policeman said with a slight accent.

"Yes."

"I am Inspector Singh. We spoke on the phone."

"Yes, I remember."

"The bodies are kept inside. There is no icebox. It is not cold."

"I understand. Please take me to them."

Namdi followed the policeman into the building. The reception area was one open space with a nurse sitting behind a large gray desk. Two corridors went off in different directions. Singh led him down the left one into a room tiled white from floor to ceiling.

On a metal gurney were the remains of a woman. The body was torn apart. The only things left were part of a leg, the ribcage, and a skull with shoulder-length blonde hair still attached. The face was gone.

Namdi's heart raced at the sight. He took out a pair of glasses from his breast pocket and put them on before approaching the gurney. "Could you hand me those rubber gloves, please?" Namdi said, pointing to a shelf loaded with supplies.

Singh took the gloves down and handed them to him.

The rubber gloves were tight and pulled on the hair of Namdi's wrist. He ignored it and reached into the woman's ribcage, looking at the marks on the bone that covered the underside. All the organs were missing and the spine was gone.

"When did you find her?"

"Two days ago."

"Where?"

"Outside a rented home. She has a husband. His two children are missing." Singh leaned back against a sink and folded his arms. "I have seen tigers there. One must have been very hungry to eat this close to the city."

"This was not a tiger," Namdi said, running the tip of his finger over deep markings carved in the bone.

"How do you know?"

"The bite marks are too large," Namdi said, flipping off his gloves and throwing them in a nearby trash bin.

"What was it then?"

Namdi put his glasses back in his pocket and stepped away from the body. "I do not know. Can you take me to the husband?"

Singh pulled out another cigarette and lit it. "Yes."

Namdi followed the police car along the bumpy road for half a mile before they turned off and drove through the edge of the plains. There were lush green bushes and immense rock formations, boulders stacked one upon the other that looked like giants in the distance. It was a hot day. Namdi had the air conditioner on full blast, but it wasn't helping. His shirt clung to him with sweat.

They pulled in front of a white house with a plaque

over the porch that read, "The Hemingway." There was a tire attached to a rope and slung over the branch of a nearby tree.

They walked up to the porch and Singh opened the front door without knocking. The interior reeked of alcohol. The television was tuned to a show in English, and a tall man in his underwear was sprawled on the couch, empty bottles of beer and vodka around him.

"Mr. Berksted," Singh said, "this is Namdi Said. He would like to talk with you." He turned to Namdi. "I will wait outside."

Namdi stood by the door, waiting for acknowledgment, but received none. He went in and moved a bottle off the couch, sitting down next to the man. "I'm very sorry," he said.

There was no response.

"If you could tell me what happened, I think we may be able to stop this from happening to others."

"I don't give a shit about others," the man mumbled.

"Maybe we could find your children?"

Berksted turned and looked at him. He had thick black bags under his eyes.

"We will find them, Mr. Berksted. But I need your help."

Tears came to his eyes and he wiped them away. "I don't know what happened. I was taking a shower and when I came out, she was gone. I found her 'cause some vultures were around."

"Did you hear anything while in the shower?"

"No, nothing. I didn't see or hear anything."

He nodded. "I will help the police with a search party and we will find your boys."

Berksted nodded and took a drink out of a bottle.

Namdi rose and walked out, stopping by the door and looking back once before leaving.

"We will need to organize a search party," Namdi said.

"Why?" Singh said. "The children could not have survived this long."

Namdi gave him a cold stare. "If it were your children, would you do it?"

"My children are dead," he said, heading back to his car. "You want to find them, look yourself."

Namdi watched as the car pulled away, kicking up puffs of dirt behind it. He turned toward the plains. Some blackbuck antelopes were grazing in the distance, their frames turning to dark shades with the range.

He got into his jeep and started the engine when the door to the house opened. Berksted stood there, wobbling from drunkenness, and looked at him.

"I could use your help," Namdi said.

Berksted went back inside the house. Namdi was about to pull away when he saw Berksted come back out, fully dressed and loading a handgun. He tucked the gun into his waistband and got in the jeep.

12

The day was boiling and all the plastic and metal in Namdi's jeep reached near-scalding temperatures. He gripped the bottom of the steering wheel with the edge of his shirt and tried not to let his arm inadvertently touch the metal gearshift.

Berksted hadn't said anything since they began driving. He stared out into the grass, watching the occasional animal go by with a cold detachment. Namdi had seen this before. When a person is murdered by another person, the family can blame the murderer. But how do you blame an animal for following its own nature?

"It was my idea to come here," Berksted finally said. "I brought them here 'cause I thought it'd be fun to go on safari and see wildlife but without all the bullshit of Africa. My wife wanted to go to Australia, but I brought them here."

"It is not your fault, Mr. Berksted."

"Isn't it?" he said, turning toward him. "How the hell would you know?"

Namdi didn't say anything.

Berksted turned back to the landscape. "Sorry," he said.

"You do not need to apologize."

A long silence followed until they turned off the dirt road and onto another one heading south.

"So you're a doctor?"

"Yes, a surgeon by specialty. But out here there are no specialties."

"You live here?"

"Sometimes. I have a house in Johannesburg in South Africa as well."

"What the hell you doin' here?"

"I spend half the year working for the government and then half the year in Johannesburg at a clinic."

Berksted took a deep breath and closed his eyes, sadness washing over him and weighing him down as surely as any weight. "The policeman said it was a tiger attack."

"I don't think so."

"What do you think it was?"

"Hyenas."

Silence for a beat. "Why do you think that?"

"Markings on the body. Hyenas are very different from other animals."

"I didn't know there were hyenas out here."

"Oh yes, they are found everywhere except North and South America. There is a lot of legends of them here and in Nepal."

Berksted was silent a moment and then said, "That's my wife, not a body."

"I apologize. In my work, it helps if I don't think of them in that way." Namdi took a sip of water out of a canteen and continued. "It is not difficult to detect hyenas, but I've never seen markings like this. They are far larger than normal hyenas. It could be a hyena with teeth deformities or some trauma to the teeth that caused it to have such specific bite patterns. But to me, it appears to be a much, much larger animal than I've seen."

Berksted looked away. There was a massive tree just off to their right and a panther sat on one of the branches, cautiously eyeing the passerby. "I used to mess around on her all the time. Blondes, brunettes, Asians... didn't matter. She didn't know. At least, I don't think she knew. She deserved better than what she got."

"We all do."

They drove in silence for the rest of the morning. They circled an area of a dozen miles, going off-road through the grass several times and stopping midday to refuel. Namdi got out and took a plastic jug of gasoline, inserting a funnel into the gas tank and pouring the fuel in. Berksted sat in the jeep, staring off into space. He was still drunk, and every once in a while would doze off.

"We can rest if you like," Namdi said.

"No, I want to keep looking."

They drove for over an hour until they reached the base of a large hill far south of the house. Vultures had gathered in a circle around a kill and were nipping at each other for position.

"Wait here," Namdi said.

He stepped out of the jeep and took a rifle from the backseat. Aiming in the air, he shot off a round and the vultures scattered as he approached. One remained, picking at whatever they had found. Namdi fired another shot and it took flight, landing on a tree a dozen yards away and watching his movements.

Namdi walked close. He lowered the rifle and put on his glasses. In front of him was a mass of rancid meat on white bones. Blood had dried into the earth and there were horns. It was the carcass of a young blackbuck. He breathed a sigh of relief and was about to return to the jeep when he heard a growl coming from a field of grass to his right.

He turned his head and saw the gold and black fur of a tiger ducked low in the tall vegetation. Tigers had distinctive growls, bassed and heavy. But they hunted by stealth. He could not see her head but had no doubt she was observing him.

Sweat rolled down his forehead into his eyes. Slowly, he backed toward the jeep, keeping a firm grip on the rifle. The jeep was more than a dozen yards away and Berksted looked half asleep.

The tiger moved. It was so subtle Namdi wouldn't have noticed if he hadn't been looking directly at her. It was just a slight adjustment in her position, going from a crouch to a tensed crouch position. She was getting ready to sprint.

Namdi darted for the jeep, hearing only a roar as the animal leaped out of the grass. He kept an eye on the ground to make sure he wouldn't trip but could hear the heavy breathing of the great cat just behind him.

He turned to look. She wasn't more than a few feet away. Her legs flexed and she pounced. She became airborne and her front paws slammed into him.

He screamed and toppled over. Berksted heard the scream and was out of the jeep and trying to steady his hand as he fired.

Namdi kept his arms over his face as the animal bit down, piercing the flesh of his forearm and scraping bone. She tugged at him, tossing him to the side as if he were a rag. The predator circled her prey, mouth oozing drool as she prepared for the killing bite to the neck, suffocating Namdi to death before beginning to eat.

Shots crackled through the air, kicking up dirt wherever they landed. The tiger yelped as she was struck in the shoulder. She dashed for the safety of the grass as Berksted continued firing until the dry click of the empty gun made him stop.

Namdi had the breath knocked out of him and his back burned from the wounds of the creature's claws. His chest felt heavy, as if her weight was still on him, and his arm was pouring blood. He ripped part of his shirt and wrapped it around the wound.

"Let's go," Berksted said, helping him up.

"My ribs are broken."

"I'll drive, come on."

With the force of a speeding truck and a gust of air that felt like a storm, Berksted was ripped from Namdi's arms. The speed at which he'd been pulled away left Namdi off balance and he fell. Namdi thought Berksted had fell. He saw him in the tall grass on his stomach, his face pale, a thick soup of saliva and black blood flowing from his mouth. Berksted screamed a wet, gurgled scream as he was dragged into the grass.

Namdi jumped to his feet and tried to run after him. He could see something moving through the grass at a quick pace, splitting apart the field like a speedboat through water. He lost sight of Berksted who was clawing at the ground to stop himself.

Berksted screamed, disappeared into the tall grass, and then there was silence.

Namdi froze in place, listening. There was the wind rustling through the brush but nothing more. It was as if the plains held its tongue. Namdi's breathing was labored and each inhalation shot pain through his ribs. As he wondered how he was going to go after Berksted, he saw something moving toward him through the grass.

It was a gray hide, spotted black. It moved with purposefulness, trying to remain quiet as a chill went down Namdi's back. He hobbled toward the jeep. The hide followed. It turned in an arc, going up away from the jeep and then coming down toward it.

Namdi started the jeep and drove, watching in his rearview. The hide was motionless a while, then ducked low and disappeared.

The sight of that hide had frightened him down to his core and he said a prayer. It hadn't moved like the tiger; it seemed to move with awareness; as if it fully understood what Namdi was thinking at that moment and tried to adjust its movements because of it. It seemed almost... human.

13

The nights in Andhra Pradesh were warm and dry as the child walked home to his village. He'd spent the day in Hyderabad hawking wooden keyrings his family made from the sycamore trees near their huts. It'd been a long day and he'd had little to eat, but he'd made more than ten dollars. Enough to feed his entire family for days.

Sometimes, when they went into the cities to buy supplies, he saw things on the television at the hotel near the store that made him wonder why some people had so much and some had so little. But mostly it was fun to see all the different shows. He would sit on the couch in the lobby and watch until the staff caught on that he wasn't with a guest and they would chase him out. But it was fun to watch people with so much food and beautiful clothes and cars. He wondered if everyone in America was always happy. Were there any sad people there?

The dirt road was narrow and surrounded by waist-high grass. The moon was only a slit in the darkness but was still enough for him to make his way without much trouble. He stopped on the side of the road to urinate.

The crickets near him were chirping loudly, and he giggled as he listened to their silly calls that filled the night.

Suddenly the crickets stopped.

The boy glanced around. It wasn't unusual for crickets to stop when people were near them, but this was different. Usually, crickets in a specific area would stop and those farther away would not. Right now, he couldn't hear anything but his own breath.

A cold chill ran down his back as he stepped away from the side of the road. He could hear the breeze rustling through the grass, but there was something else as well. A muffled crunching of the bushes. The sound was soft, but it was loud enough for him to hear. He looked down the road and saw the outline of the first hut of his village.

He walked quickly, telling himself it was only the sounds of the earth. He'd walked this same route hundreds of times and nothing had happened. The larger predators stayed away from people. He had nothing to be afraid of. His father had walked this route and his father before him. This was their road.

There was another sound behind him. The boy couldn't tell where it came from. It seemed to come from the wind and swirl around in the grass before going to the sky. His heart was beating faster now. He looked once toward his village and then behind him. Making his decision, he sprinted for his hut.

There was a ruckus behind him, grass and weeds being torn from their roots as something crashed through the brush in pursuit.

He was now dashing with all his strength, his legs burning and his breath hot like the air around him. The sounds had grown louder; it was right behind him.

The boy was close to the first hut. It was two stories and made of wood and straw. He burst through the wooden door and saw a man and woman sitting by a small fire. He'd seen them before; they were friends of his mother.

Before he could say anything, a roar rattled the hut, shaking the beams and causing dirt and straw to fly off the roof. The boy looked to the man whose eyes were wide. He grabbed his wife and took the boy's arm and ran to the back of the hut, where a small ladder led to the second floor. He took his wife by the hips and helped her up as she climbed and disappeared into the darkness. The man then helped the boy up. The wife held him in her arms as the man yelled not to come down.

There was another growl, then dirt being kicked up near the walls. Heavy breathing circled the hut and was followed by clawing against the wood. Whatever was outside was looking for a way in.

More dirt and more digging and then the boy heard the man gasp. There was the deafening splinter of wood, and then laughter. Awful laughter like he had never heard.

He jumped for the ladder and started to climb. The boy could see his head poke through the second-floor opening before there was more laughter, and then the man screamed. The wife took hold of the man, but he was ripped away from her and pulled down to the first floor. A warm spatter of blood hit her face.

The screams and crunching of bones made the boy start to cry. Then the noise stopped. The wife had stopped screaming and sat in shock, trembling. She let go of the boy and kicked the ladder down before scooting to a wall away from the opening. The boy began to go over to her, and froze when he looked down through the opening.

Dark black blood stained the ground and the walls. The man's body was not there, but bits of flesh mixed with the dirt appeared like giant insects on the dry earth. There was a growl, and the boy jumped backward. As he sat in the woman's arms, they screamed for help, pounding against the walls, tears running down their cheeks.

The wood creaked. Both of them listened breathlessly. The hut shook again and bent, the woman screaming as she realized the shelter was collapsing. It shook only a few more seconds before a thundering sound filled the boy's ears and he fell with the collapsing building and crashed into the ground.

The woman's screams stopped and the boy couldn't see what was happening with blood dripping into his eyes. His head was cut and he felt the sharp pressure of a break in his leg. Then he felt something hot against the skin on his arms.

It was breath.

14

In some places, the Indian Ocean was black as tar and in others a shining turquoise blue. The third-largest body of water on earth, it has highly important sea routes connecting the Americas with the Middle East, India and Asia. The traffic is mostly petroleum from the Middle East on its way to the United States, though hydrocarbons in the ocean floor itself are being tapped more often.

Eric thought to be over such a vast expanse of water and nothing else felt like tight-rope walking without a net; one slip and it would lead to your death. But the beauty of the water wasn't lost on him. Something about the sea could make him forget everything else. Looking at it from high above, he felt that it'd always been a part of him, each wave like an emotion flowing through him.

The plane ride had been long and claustrophobic. He and Thomas went from luxury planes on Air Asia to rickety private planes in India that rattled and shook at high speeds. Their pilot out of Calcutta had been drunk but had flown more competently than some of the sober ones. There were only a handful of people on the plane from the port of Goa to Andhra Pradesh, most of them laborers being sent to this or that mine to slave for little wages.

More than once, Eric had thought to himself, *What the hell am I doing here?* In Goa, he considering catching a flight back to the States but decided to get away from everything for at least a little while, if nothing else, would make the trip worthwhile. It was here he met Thomas' assistant, Jalani. Tall and with dreadlocks and muscular arms, she reminded him of an Amazonian warrior. She had asked him what he was doing here, and he explained what Thomas had said about revenge. She laughed and said that was just something he said. More than likely, he just felt guilty that James had died on one of his guided trips, and wanted to make up for it by taking Eric under his wing.

Flying over Andhra Pradesh, he could see the great gold and green plains, the thick shrubbery of the bush, and the ancient trees with leafy branches hanging down to the ground. Wildlife of all shapes and colors painted the landscape, and the skies were ruled by the black vultures, their bald heads tucked into their shoulders. Occasionally a village would pass beneath them. They looked much like the shantytowns of Depression-era America; rusted tin buildings with mud and straw filling any gaps. On the outskirts of the villages were the less developed buildings made wholly of mud or straw or wood bound together with rope or vine. The mountains ranged from small green hills to giants with cloud-covered peaks. It felt like he was stepping into a lost world.

The airport was smaller, with only a few runways, but he could sense the international flavor of the nation from this tiny corner of it: abstract architectural designs donated by the Dutch; a few trucks with BMW logos hauling cargo next to Mercedes Benz dump-trucks. There was a British bistro situated near one of the terminals along with a free car service to the local British-owned hotels.

Thomas stepped off the plane first and Eric followed. The air was salty because of the proximity of the ocean, but it was warm and comfortable. Eric walked across the tarmac, a canvas bag filled with his clothes slung over his shoulder. Jalani walked next to him, smiling.

"You're glad you're here?" Eric asked.

"Yes. I love India. It's not Africa, but it's close. Do you miss home?"

"I don't know. I think I needed a little break. Might be good for me."

She raised her brows. "I don't think you'll find hunting out here to be much of a relaxing break."

They walked through the main terminal. The interior was blue carpet with a stained white ceiling and blue chairs bolted to the walls for the waiting passengers to use. Eric was impressed with how modern it looked considering the savage plains and jungles practically right outside the door.

Out on the curb in front of the airport was a waiting car with a driver in large sunglasses, chewing on a toothpick. Thomas acknowledged him as he went to the trunk and put in his bag.

Eric rode in the backseat with Jalani while Thomas was up front with the driver. They were speaking in a language Eric couldn't understand, but every once in a while they would laugh or tell particularly long stories. The car was zipping down a long stretch of highway near the coast, and the sun was bright in a cloudless sky. Eric stared out the window in wonder. The ocean and sky surrounding them appeared crystal blue. They drove for less than two miles before coming to the town of Kavali. It resembled a modern city but rundown. Except for the tourist areas, the homes and buildings were timeworn, the metal rusted and the paint peeling off the wood. Some of the houses had red tile roofs, and others were just cheap tin from top to bottom.

"You have to be careful," Jalani said in her perfect English, her sixth language, Thomas had informed him. "This is an impoverished area. And when people are poor, they do things they may not otherwise do."

Eric could see an old building that looked like a destroyed castle next to the shore. Jalani noticed his curiosity and said, "It's a fort. Four hundred years old and built by Muslims. It has a history of violence and death. People here say it curses its owner."

"It doesn't look so bad."

Thomas answered, "Nothing on the outside tells what's on the inside, does it?"

Soon they were off the highway and in downtown Kavali, a place Jalani called the old part of Kavali. The architecture was a mixture of Hindu and Arabic and many of the merchants crowding the narrow, winding streets were wearing traditional Hindu garb. The buildings didn't go above four or five stories, and they were mostly a dull white with various colored awnings and flags from nations across the world hung over windows.

"It's always been like this," Jalani said. "Crowded. Children come here and sell things made for the tourists."

"What do they make?"

"Little shapes out of wood. Animal shapes. The tourists buy it for their children. Hyderabad—that's the capital of this region—it's crowded too. But it doesn't have the same feeling of Kavali."

The car stopped in front of a square building with a British flag hanging down from the roof. The driver shook Thomas's hand and they said goodbye as everyone climbed out.

The weather was wet, hot, and relentless. It made it difficult to breathe. Eric grabbed his bag and followed Thomas into the building.

From the uniforms the front desk staff was wearing it was apparent it was a hotel. Bagboys promptly took their bags, and Thomas tipped them. He motioned for Eric to step outside with him.

Thomas stood by the door and took out his pipe, lighting it and inhaling the smoke deeply before speaking. "There is something about India that can penetrate the soul. It's a mystical place, boy. Life teems here like nowhere else on earth." He took a puff of the pipe and looked back to Jalani who was speaking with the front desk receptionist. "The language is Telugu here, but everyone speaks English. You should have no trouble getting around."

"You leaving somewhere?"

"Um hm, I have business to attend to tonight. We'll be traveling with three clients and I have to organize their arrival. Jalani will stay with you and show you the sights." He pulled out some rupees and handed them to Eric. "Relax and enjoy yourself; this city can be quite fun. I'll see you tomorrow." He turned to walk away and then stopped and looked at Eric again. "Stay in the city, Eric. Don't travel anywhere outside its limits. Death is around every corner here."

15

After he'd visited his room and brushed his teeth, which he hadn't done in almost thirty hours, Eric took to walking the streets. The roads were well paved, but the sidewalks were uneven, and parts were made of cobblestones which, though charming, hurt his feet and ankles. The smells of the city were amazing; a mix of Hindu spices from the open markets, sweet vegetables broiling over spits, honey-tea coming from the tea houses, and the salt of the ocean air.

There was a café not more than a block from the hotel. Eric sat on the patio and ordered a coffee from a slim woman with caramel skin. It was brought back with sugar, some milk, and a little powdery chocolate on a separate dish. As he drank, he watched the hordes of people moving through the street. The people here didn't have a sense of urgency. There were no honking car horns or angry shouting.

Though the heat was boiling, many of the women wore the traditional Hindu headscarves but weren't sweating. They were working harder than the men, selling handmade items or carrying massive jugs of water or food. Most of them had children by their sides. Some of them smiled and nodded hello to Eric, but most ignored him. He got the feeling that there was an implicit agreement between the street hawkers and the restaurants that they would not hassle the customers while they were eating.

Eric stayed at the café well into the afternoon, ordering a dish of lamb with yogurt sauce for dinner. The people were friendly and he struck up a conversation with some New Zealand tourists that sat at the table next to him. They informed him that the lamb was actually made from a vegetarian paste. There were apparently only a handful of places in the city one could get freshly cooked meat.

As the sun began its descent and the sky went pink and gold, Jalani came to the café and sat next to him.

"I have a special treat for you," she said.

"Oh yeah? What?"

"It's a surprise."

They left the café and made their way down a winding street, past hawkers that crowded around Eric, trying to sell him wooden key rings and wallets and handmade flutes.

"Mahogany!" one of the merchants yelled as he held a flute in Eric's face.

Jalani said, "It's not mahogany, it's painted."

They walked down a few more blocks and took a turn through a long alleyway between two old apartment buildings. A jeep was waiting for them and they climbed in and drove to the beach. Jalani gave him a bathing suit she had with her and they both changed in the bathrooms. When they emerged, they were near a golden sand beach. There was a wooden pier jutting out into the sea and Jalani headed for it, not waiting for Eric.

Eric could see a canoe lashed to the pier. There were two oars and some chains next to a cooler inside the canoe.

The water was stilling for the coming evening. The sunlight reflected off of it a bright orange as they walked to the end of the pier and Jalani motioned for Eric to climb into the canoe.

"Where we going?" Eric said.

"Don't worry, you'll enjoy it."

Eric climbed in and sat in the back as Jalani took the front. She grabbed an oar and unlashed from the pier before paddling out into the vast expanse of water. Eric took the other oar and tried to keep rhythm but found Jalani was paddling too fast and gave up the effort.

When they were a hundred yards from shore, Jalani stopped paddling and looked around at the murky water. Her eyes were slits and her brow furrowed from concentration as she stared into the depths, though Eric couldn't see more than a few feet below the surface. Jalani opened the cooler. There was a fat chicken inside, its feathers plucked and with dried blood crusted to it. She stabbed a large iron hook through it and attached the hook to a thin chain. She then tied the chain to the front of the canoe and threw the chicken overboard. Eric was about to say something, but Jalani stopped him with a motion of her hand and they sat in silence.

Finally, a streak of gray broke through the surface a dozen feet from the boat: the dorsal fin of a shark. It was swimming in a full arch around the canoe, the peak of its tailfin sticking out of the water about four feet behind its dorsal fin.

"Holy shit," Eric said.

"Take the ropes."

Eric looked down and saw two ropes wound in tight circles attached to the canoe with bolts. He grabbed them and held on. "What are we—"

"Keep quiet!"

The shark was as long as a car. There was splashing behind them. Eric turned to see another shark approaching, its skin gray-brown in the sunlight. It swam near the chicken and Jalani pulled up on the chain and hauled the chicken back in the canoe until the shark swam around to the other side.

"Jalani, what the hell are we doing?"

"He wasn't big enough."

"Big enough for what?"

There was more splashing and more fins, about five of them. They were circling the canoe and taking small bites in the cloud of blood the chicken carcass gave off. But every time one of them would come in to feed, Jalani would pull the carcass back onto the canoe.

Suddenly there was a commotion as the sharks banked away from the canoe, swimming into the depths. The water stilled and the ocean went silent. Eric glanced around. Even the smaller fish that had come by earlier to have a look at the carcass had vanished. There was nothing.

"Watch," Jalani said.

Eric had gone from nervousness to fear and was gripping the ropes so tightly it hurt his hands. As he let go to examine them, the canoe lurched forward, throwing him back and nearly over the side. Jalani reached out and grabbed his shirt collar, bringing him into place. Something had the carcass and was pulling at the line.

The canoe stopped moving. The only sound now was Eric's heavy breathing. Before he could say anything, the canoe jerked forward and then tilted to the side, nearly submerging the two of them. Jalani was squealing with delight, laughing as the water splashed onto her face. Eric thought she sounded insane.

The canoe was spinning slowly now; whatever was underneath was circling. It began heading out farther into the sea, pulling them along.

"Unhook the damn line!" Eric shouted.

The pulling of the canoe slowed and then stopped. Eric could see a large mass coming up from the deep. The water was parting as the creature made its way to the surface just off the port side of the canoe. He noticed the dorsal fin first, about two feet high and silver-gray, then the tail, and the monstrous head with pitch-black eyes and jagged white teeth. It was a great white shark.

The shark was circling them, the hook jutting through the flesh of its mouth. It was at least as large as the canoe, about twelve feet, and Eric got the impression that the canoe would crumble if it decided to attack.

The enormous fish swam slowly, its circles gradually decreasing as it approached the canoe. It was tilted slightly to the side and its black eye was kept steady on them, staring. Finally, the shark passed only a few feet away, and Eric saw its terrible mouth as it opened, taking in the residual blood in the water. When it was near enough, to Eric's shock, Jalani slammed the oar into the shark's snout.

The pain made the shark thrash violently from side-to-side and then shoot away. The canoe followed as Jalani laughed. The shark was in a frenzy now. It was lashing its powerful body left and right and the canoe was beingthrown one way and then the other as if caught in a storm.

The shark dove. The canoe followed; its front end completely submerging as it was being pulled down. It started going vertical and Jalani unhooked the chain, the canoe slapping back horizontally on the water.

Jalani looked back to Eric with a big smile, water dripping from her soaking hair into her eyes. Silently, she picked up an oar and began paddling back to the pier.

"How was it?" she asked.

Eric collapsed onto his back, his heart feeling like it was about to tear out of his chest. "I think I'd like to go back to the café, please."

16

Night over Kavali was starless and the air had the humid warmth that foretold a coming rainstorm. The merchants had packed up and gone home, but hawkers still stood on street corners and in dark alleyways. Some of the hawkers were families, each child taking turns selling as the parents smoked hashish or drank in cheap bars.

There was a bar across the street from Eric's hotel and he sat at the outdoor patio at a round wooden table, outdoor gas lamps giving a dim illumination around him. He sipped at a beer, and when it was done, he felt the fatigue in his muscles from the journey and decided to sleep.

As he rose to leave, he saw Thomas walk out of the hotel with another man. The man was dressed in shorts and a T-shirt with an enormous belly bulging out from underneath. He had a black beard, curly hair, and appeared Greek with his olive skin. The men walked over and came to Eric's table. Thomas sat down and the man went to the bar to order drinks.

"So I believe you've had quite an eventful day," Thomas said with a smirk.

"Did you know she was going to do that?"

"More or less."

"I could've died."

"You drive in a one-ton steel cage every day with other people on the road in one-ton steel cages speeding by you, some of them angry or drunk or insane, and you're worried about a fish?" Thomas took out his pipe and lit it with some matches. "Besides, sharks—especially the great white—don't enjoy the taste of human flesh. They only attack us out of mistake, despite the myths surrounding them.

"But it wasn't a joyride, you know. It was a ritual, a type of conquering of the sea. Many of the fishermen here had to do it while they were apprenticing. They do something similar where Jalani's from. I was surprised she took you with her; she must really like you."

The other man came back with two large drinks and sat down. He had a joyous look on his face and already appeared drunk.

"This is Douglas Patsinakis," Thomas said. "He'll be going on the hunt with us."

"Pleased to meet you," Douglas said with a wide grin. He held up his drink in salute. "Here's to the hunt," he said before guzzling half the glass. He finished and smacked his lips almost comically before wiping his mouth. "So how long have you been hunting?" he asked Eric.

"This'll be my first time."

"Really? I wish I was a virgin again. The sights and smells of the plains and the Pradeshian jungle are like nowhere else. I don't even mind the heat when I'm out chasing a kill. You can lose yourself in it. It's a damn good time." He turned to Thomas. "So this monster of yours is a real man-eater, eh?"

"So it seems."

"I killed a man-eater in Tsavo once. A lion. They had those two other man-eaters there, oh, when was that… more than a century ago. I would've loved to have been there. Together they killed about a hundred and forty people, the devils."

"If rumor is to be believed," Thomas said, "this one will kill more."

"You think so?" Douglas said. "One animal?"

"Probably not. Stories do tend to get aggrandized in this part of the world rather quickly."

"Well," Douglas said, pausing to take a drink, "I hope the bastard's a big one. But I was under the impression that you saw it, Thomas?"

"It was dark so I can't attest perfectly to its size, but it was certainly large."

Douglas finished his drink and leaned back. "Damn good." He looked at Eric. "So what's your name, my friend?"

"Eric."

"Well Eric, let me tell you something about hunting; not everyone can do it. Everyone thinks they can but they can't. When you're face-to-face with a lion, you have to dig down deep inside you to pull that trigger. They have a savage beauty about them and their eyes stare into you if you let them. You really see where you are on the food chain when a lion's staring at you with those eyes."

"He'll do fine," Thomas said.

"Sure, maybe. Everyone's got a plan in a fight until they get punched, right?" Douglas looked to them both and then nodded as he stood up. "Well, I'm going to get drunk. Or drunker I should say."

Eric waited until Douglas was out of earshot and then said, "This sounds dangerous, Thomas. You sure you should be taking other people with us?"

He shrugged. "Everyone's a killer. Might as well make some money from them while I can."

Eric leaned back in the chair, glancing once to the moon, which was a crescent of silver in the sky. "You ever killed a person?"

"Why would you ask that?"

"I don't know. You seem like the kind of person that has."

He took a long pull from the pipe and then put out the embers before tucking it back into his pocket. "No. But I nearly killed a man in Venice once. The city has a history of such bloodshed I suppose, so it wasn't so out of place. But it is such a beautiful city. I regret that I may never be able to go back."

"What happened?"

"I was in love. A woman from a little town in Sicily. She sold fruit on the side of the road near my flat and I used to buy something from her every morning. I haven't committed an act of courage so great as using broken Italian to ask her to dinner. She loved me, too, I think. But I certainly loved her."

"You tried to kill her?"

"No," Thomas said, looking off at a group of tourists, "her husband."

"Oh."

Thomas blinked a few times and inhaled a deep breath as if the action cleared the thoughts from his mind.

He looked over to Douglas, who was flirting with some older American tourists. Thomas rose and put his hand on Eric's shoulder. "Get rested. Tomorrow you'll become a hunter."

17

Eric's room was uncomfortably hot during the night and the squeaks of mammoth cockroaches were coming from the corners. The sun rose and quickly filled the room with flowing light, making it impossible to sleep. Eric was groggy, but he stood up and stretched before looking out the window and seeing two green topless jeeps parked on the curb in front of the hotel. Some locals were loading them with suitcases and coolers and giant plastic jugs of water.

Eric dressed and went down to the first-floor bathroom. When he was done with his toiletries, he went to the small cafeteria and saw Thomas sitting with Douglas and two new faces. One of them was a man wearing a corduroy jacket with sunglasses pushed up into his black hair. The other was a woman, blonde and petite wearing tight stretch pants and a black blouse revealing a little cleavage.

Eric took a plate from a small buffet table and loaded it with eggs and toast before getting a cup of coffee and sitting down at Thomas's table.

Thomas said, "How was your night?"

"Didn't sleep much. It's so hot I always feel dehydrated."

"You have to constantly drink water and limit your sodium while here." He turned to the couple seated across from him. "This is Eric," he said.

"Hey," the man said with a warm smile. "I'm Will and this is my wife Sandra."

Eric nodded hello and they exchanged pleasantries. The familiarity with which they greeted him made him suspect Thomas had already mentioned him.

"So where are you from, Eric?" Will said.

"New Hampshire."

"Oh yeah? We live in Boston. I manage to get up to New Hampshire every autumn for the leaves. Beautiful state."

Thomas said, "Will's a brilliant businessman and hunter."

Will chuckled. "Well, not too shitty anyway."

Thomas said, "He was actually working on becoming a priest when his hormones got the better of him."

Douglas said, "You were going to be a priest? Why on earth would you do that?"

"Oh, thought I could do some good serving God, I guess."

Douglas scoffed. "All nonsense if you ask me. I've seen all manner of cruelties and very little compassion in the world. Doesn't seem to point to a God."

"Maybe you're not looking in the right places," Will said with a wry smile.

One of the men loading the jeeps came in and said something to Thomas. He nodded and stood up. "The jeeps are ready. If you'd care to gather your things, we'll be leaving within the hour. And if you'll excuse me, I have a few things to attend to before we go." He bowed his head slightly to Sandra. "Madame."

She smiled.

"I'll come too," Douglas said, sopping up the last of his eggs with a croissant and shoving it into his mouth. "Haven't really gotten to see the town yet."

"Of course," Thomas said, not taking his eyes of Sandra. "Have you had a chance to see the town?" he said to her.

"No, not really."

"It wouldn't do any harm if you'd like to accompany us. I have to go down the shore a bit and it is a beautiful drive."

"Go ahead, honey," Will said.

"You don't want to come?"

"No, you go. Have fun."

"All right," she said.

As they walked out, Will was watching his wife and had a glimmer in his eye. His deep love for her was written on his face.

"She's quite lovely, isn't she?" Will said.

"Yeah."

"I ask the Lord sometimes why he blessed me with her. She's a wonderful woman, full of life." He took a bite of eggs and washed it down with cold juice. "You married Eric?"

"No."

"Huh. Just never met the right woman or you just too young?"

"I don't think marriage is in my future. Don't want to be tied down." He grinned. "Thomas told me on the plane ride over here that love is something invented by chocolate companies for Valentine's Day."

He chuckled. "That sounds like him. But don't listen to him. You should fall in love. As many times as you can. Love makes up in height what it lacks in length. Frost said that somewhere I think."

Eric bit into his eggs; they were rubbery and he put down his fork and tried to remove the taste with coffee. "So what made you leave being a priest?"

"Sex, what else? Who the hell can be celibate their entire lives? Might as well be in the grave already. But it did have some interesting aspects." He shrugged. "Worked out for the best."

He finished his food and pushed his plate away before taking out a cigar. "Only smoke 'em on vacation. This stuff will kill ya. But I guess, according to Thomas, everything out here will kill ya."

18

Eric strolled around the town with Will for almost an hour, haggling with the hawkers and buying little wooden trinkets for less than a dollar. They stopped at a café and had some ice cream, the scoops melting into thick syrup from the heat almost before they were served.

When they returned to the hotel, the jeeps were fully packed and Thomas, Sandra, and Douglas stood next to one talking. Jalani was checking everything in both vehicles, her brow heavy with sweat. She saw Eric and grinned.

"You'll be riding with me today," she said.

"We going to be smacking tigers with oars this time?"

"Maybe. Depends if you annoy me or not."

Jalani climbed into the second jeep as Thomas and Douglas went to the first. Sandra pointed to them, and Will nodded before jumping into the passenger seat next to Jalani. Eric stepped up into the backseat. It was cramped because of all the supplies loaded behind him, but there was a cooler full of ice and bottled water next to him, and he took some of the ice and slid it over his face and neck.

The jeeps rumbled to life. Douglas was driving the other one, Thomas sitting next to him smoking his pipe with his boots up on the dashboard, appearing like a nineteenth-century aristocrat in his full canvas garb. They began slowly winding through the neighborhood, honking at the diverse crowds that gathered in the street to talk or conduct business. Soon, they were out of downtown Kavali and heading north on the highway.

The ocean quickly became a distant glimmer behind them as they moved farther inland. Will and Jalani were discussing the colonial history of Andhra Pradesh. Will seemed genuinely interested, aptly paying attention to anything Jalani said.

After a few hours, they steered away from the highway and onto a wide dirt road. Around them, the grass—gold, and dark green—became waist-high and thick. The trees were growing denser and large boulders and rock formations were beginning to appear.

"Do you know what the animal is?" Will asked Jalani.

"Hyenas."

"I heard it was possibly a rogue tiger."

"Maybe."

Within a short time, they were dozens of miles away from any type of civilization. There was only sky and grass and trees. A herd of Asian elephants was slowly crossing their path. Douglas stopped in front of them, laughing at the sight of it all. He brought out a flask and took a long drink before passing it to Thomas and Sandra.

It took less than three hours for Eric to feel sunburnt and dehydrated. He guzzled water from the frosty bottles and constantly rubbed sunblock on his face and arms. Jalani hardly did anything; the heat didn't seem to bother her at all.

"There's a village down a few kilometers," Jalani said. "We can eat there."

The village was nothing more than a few huts placed around a large pit used for fires. The inhabitants were a dark black with ornate jewelry and red and yellow cloth wrapped around them for clothing, dark red markings in the center of their foreheads. Their feet were dry and cracked with inch-thick calluses from their toes to their heel. Children gathered around the jeeps as they parked a couple dozen feet away. Jalani said harsh words to scatter them and then laughed softly.

"I remember when I was here last," Jalani said, "this village had no money. Nothing from the modern world. Now they have cigarettes and liquor and rifles. They've only taken what's bad about the modern world."

Thomas and Jalani went to greet some of the elders, and Eric stayed by the jeeps with Will and Sandra. He saw Will wrap his arm around her and she pulled away and leaned against the jeep.

Eventually, Jalani waved them over and they all sat in a circle around the pit as some of the tribal women lit a fire. They had killed a lamb recently and, in honor of their guests, were going to cook it with roots and potatoes. Eric sat next to Jalani and listened to the sing-songy language. It had beautiful upward inflections which gave a wholly different sound from any language he'd ever heard.

"I didn't know tribes like this existed in India," Eric said.

"Not many are left. But there are a few," Jalani said. "They live the same as they did a thousand years ago and refuse to go to the cities for anything."

One of the elders spoke for a bit and Thomas spoke with him. He spit into the fire and turned to Douglas. "This elder says he's seen our monster, but he doesn't know what it is."

"How did he see it?" Douglas asked.

"They lost one of their tribe a couple of weeks ago."

"Maybe we should get a tracker if they could spare someone."

Thomas asked and the elder shook his head and said something harsh.

"What's the matter?" Douglas asked.

"They're scared. They say this animal can't be killed."

"Why not?"

"They think it's a demon."

"A demon?" Douglas said with a grin. "Well, assure them it is only an animal and one that we intend to get rid of."

"One of the children claims that it spoke with them."

"Nonsense. Tell them we're willing to pay for the services of a good tracker and that I will not stop until this beast is dead. If you explain it in terms of self-interest, they'll understand."

Thomas spoke and the man thought a while, then said something and offered his hand. He shook it and they held each other for a moment. "He agrees," Thomas said, "but not for money. He says only because we are serious and he does not wish any more of his tribe to die. He also invites us to stay the night."

"Tell him that's very gracious. I think we should accept, Thomas."

"As do I. They'll be insulted if we don't. Besides, he says sometimes at night they can hear the laughter of the demon."

Eric found the people of the tribe friendly and wel-
coming. Anything they had, they shared. When darkness
fell, they lit fires and ate fresh lamb, which was greasy
but had a slightly sweet taste that he found appealing.
The villagers were not vegetarians like most of the population of India, and they ate heartily along with them.
Afterward Thomas shared some beers with the elders
and they sat around telling stories. Eric wandered off
to the outskirts of the village, standing on the edge of
the green shrubbery and golden fields. The wind rustled
through the plains in a soft whisper, almost like it was
speaking. It was enough to send a chill down his back.

"Beautiful, isn't it?" Will said as he walked up and
stood next to him. "I don't think I've ever seen a sky so
dark."

Eric watched the grass. "I like these people. They
seem more innocent than us."

"I doubt that, Eric. We all have the capacity for evil
inside us. Even them."

Eric picked a long strand of grass and twirled it in his
fingers, looking out into the fields at some deer grazing
near them on the open plains. "Why'd you come here,
Will?"

"Vacation."

"You hunt man-eating animals for a vacation?"

Will smiled. "No. My wife is friends with Thomas. I
think they went to school together in Europe. He offered
a once in a lifetime trip and she insisted we come. I
don't think she likes Boston very much, so we're always
zipping off to somewhere." Will took out his cigars and

handed one to Eric before lighting it and taking one for himself.

Eric took a puff and glanced up to the moon. "This thing killed my father."

Will was silent a while. "I know. I'm sorry." He smoked for a few moments in silence. "So is that why you're here? Revenge?"

"Yes."

He shrugged. "Good as reason as any I guess. It won't help, though. It never does."

"Gentleman!" Thomas yelled out, "it's insulting to be apart from the group during a feast."

Will put his hand on Eric's shoulder. "Let's get drunk."

As they walked back to the group, Jalani handed them a large bowl filled with a rancid, fermented drink. Will took a long swig and gave it to Eric. The tribe lit a large bonfire, making it roar with dry timber and moss. They pulled out a few drums and began a dance, chanting a melody that Sandra and Thomas took up as well. Soon, they were all drunk and dancing and singing songs that would last well into the night.

Jalani would glance over to Eric and smile. Eventually, she came up and sat next to him.

"How do you feel?" she asked.

"Fine."

She smiled. "You looked like you were about to faint in that canoe."

"Not my finest moment, no."

"These tribes think animals are just their ancestors in a different form."

Eric smiled.

"You think their beliefs funny?" Jalani said playfully.

"No, it just amazes me the things people like to believe."

Jalani glanced over at the group. They were all around the fire, dancing and singing in melody to the music. "Will you dance?" she said. She stood up and motioned for him to follow.

Eric stood up and followed her close to the flames. Her slender figure appeared exotic next to the fire, her silhouette sleek and thin; darkness against flame. Her dance wasn't like the others' drunken movements. She was purposeful, her hips moving in line with her legs and her muscular upper body. She took Eric's hands and wrapped them around her hips. When they were coated in sweat and their muscles were warm and stretched from the movement, she leaned in and kissed him.

Suddenly, she pulled away.

"What?" Eric said.

She looked out over the plains, her eyes narrowing. "I thought I heard something."

"What?"

She stared out over the tall grass in silence for a long time.

"Jalani? What'd you hear?"

"It sounded like… laughter."

19

Dawn over the plains began with a smoke-gray sky. Soon, the red and orange of the sun would come over the mountains and paint the landscape with color. Then the heat would begin. The waves would come up off the ground creating mirages in every direction Eric looked. The smell of warm grass and dirt filled his nostrils.

Eric awoke in a tent next to Jalani and Douglas. Douglas had snored like a bear the entire night, but Eric was so tired he had fallen right to sleep. Jalani had slept against him, her body warm through the night. He gently removed her hand from his chest before he climbed out of the tent into the bright day. The tribe was up and around. He noticed that the men were gone and only the women and children remained. Some of the children giggled as he made a face at them.

Thomas was seated on the ground, leaning against a tree near one of the tents and sipping some tea. He nodded hello to Eric as he sat in the shade next to him.

"Quite a sociable people, no?" Thomas said.

"I like 'em."

"Sleep well?"

"Not bad, but I was pretty drunk. What was that drink anyway?"

"Goat milk and rotten oranges mixed with the spit of all the tribe and then left to ferment in the sun."

Eric's face must've done something because Thomas laughed.

"You'll be fine," Thomas said. "But feel free to ask me what something is before you eat or drink it." He looked out over the tall grass as a wave of wind blew, furiously shaking the trees around them. "So what do you think of Andhra Pradesh?"

"It's beautiful. I can see why my dad came here."

Thomas took a sip of tea. "Your father died not far from here, maybe two or three day's journey." He paused. "He saved my life. He distracted the animal from me and… well, anyway, I owe him a great deal."

Will crawled out of a tent on the far side of the village and waved hello as he stretched his back.

"How do you know Will and his wife?" Eric asked.

"I attended school with Sandra. We were, at that time, quite the item."

"Shit Thomas, is there anyone you haven't slept with?"

He smiled. "It didn't last long. It never does."

"What happened?"

"I moved away and she didn't want to leave London. I couldn't stay; it was getting a bit tight for me. I needed breathing space."

Sandra came out of the tent after Will. She was wearing shorts and the tan smoothness of her legs made Thomas stare a bit longer than he should've. She walked over, a smile parting her pink lips.

"Hello boys," Sandra said playfully. "Ready for your big manly kill today?"

"Oh," Thomas said, "I don't believe we'll get her so quick. If it is just a *her* and not a clan."

"Big Thomas," she said, "always on the hunt. You know, Eric, he was a ladykiller back when we were in college. All the girls thought he was so tough and mysterious."

"Tough, yes," Thomas said with a grin, "though I can't attest to how mysterious I am." They looked at each other a moment, and then Thomas said, "We should probably get moving soon, don't want to waste any daylight."

"Where are all the men?" Eric asked.

"Hunting. Some of the women stay and tend to the children and the rest go foraging." He stood up and wiped some dirt off his pants. "Let's eat something and get going."

After a quick breakfast of coffee and eggs cooked over an open fire, the jeeps were off again. Next to Eric in the backseat of the second jeep sat a tracker from the tribe. He was wiry and had an intense glare in his charcoal eyes. A rifle sat next to him and he didn't remove his hand from it for a second.

Eric thought it odd that Sandra only traveled with Thomas and even stranger that Will didn't mind.

"Where we going?" Eric asked Jalani.

"There was a killing yesterday near another village. If they still have the body, we're going to see it."

"Why?"

"We can tell what type of animal it is from the way they kill."

The day dragged on and the driving was difficult as

the road turned into a rough path that few cars had driven down before. The grass was growing again over the trail and the earth was now fine red dirt, almost like sand. Eric took inventory of the supplies while they drove: the second jeep had all the food and water and the first was loaded with the gasoline. He wasn't sure the food could last more than a week for this many people.

At the base of a large green hill was another village. This one was larger than the last and had some of the tin huts made from scavenged metal found in the plains. The people dressed and looked different from those of the other village even though they were only a few hours away from each other. There was a monkey tied to a post near the edge of the village, and a group of children were throwing food at it, their laughter a welcome sound after hours of nothing but roaring jeep engines and wind.

The jeeps parked near the children and one of the boys ran back to the village and into one of the huts. A few moments later, a man emerged with him. He was dressed in a dirty blue button-up shirt and jeans. He smiled widely as he saw Thomas approaching.

"Namdi?" Thomas said.

They shook hands and Namdi looked over the group. "Dangerous for tourists here, no?" he said.

"Special group," Thomas said.

Namdi saw Jalani and nodded. "How are you, Jalani?"

"Good, Doctor. You?"

"Fine. What are you still doing with this old man?"

"He pays too much to kill him."

Namdi laughed. Thomas turned to the rest of the group and said, "This is Doctor Namdi Said, an old friend. This is Eric, Sandra, Will and Douglas."

Namdi bowed his head. "Pleased to meet you."

"So," Thomas said, "you still haven't answered my question. I thought you'd be in Johannesburg this time of year."

"I was doing some contract work for the government here when I came across the injuries. They led me here."

"What injuries?"

Namdi gave him a puzzled look and then said, "Follow me."

Thomas looked at Eric, "Come with me. The rest of you wait here."

They walked through the village, Eric lagging a little behind as he watched the faces of the people that peeked out of doorways to steal a glance at him. Many of them looked frightened and the rest looked aggressive. One small boy pointed at him and said something as he walked past.

"Actually," Thomas said, "I was told you have a body, Namdi."

"We have many bodies."

"Fresh one from two nights ago. I'd like to see that."

Namdi nodded.

They walked from the village heading south into the brush. Thomas explained to Eric that the dead were kept away from the village in case their smell attracted scavengers. In the middle of a thicket of green bushes was a path cut out that led to a tin shack. Namdi opened the door which had a padlock on it.

Inside was the corpse of a man, or at least what Eric thought was a man. He had to glance away and prepare himself before looking again.

Thomas looked at Namdi and said, "The family hasn't asked to bury him yet?"

"They don't bury the dead here," Namdi said. "Hyenas

dig up and eat corpses. We burn the dead each night."

Thomas spoke softly and laid his hand on Eric's shoulder. "Go get Jalani."

Eric jogged through the village, watching the crowds of children giggling as he went by. Some of them appeared somber and averted their eyes.

He saw his group drinking water and eating beef jerky by the jeeps. He called to Jalani and they walked back together

"What's the matter?" Jalani said.

"I've, um, never actually seen a dead body before."

"It's no different than a dead animal. You've seen that before, haven't you?"

"No, Jalani. It's a lot different."

Jalani went into the shack and froze. She stared at the corpse a while before looking at Thomas. Eric watched them but didn't understand what was going on. The body looked like he expected someone to look like after being eaten by a tiger or hyenas, or a bear or whatever the hell this was.

"Is this fresh?" Jalani asked.

Thomas nodded and then walked out of the shack without saying anything. Eric followed.

"I don't understand," Eric said.

"You didn't notice the color of the flesh? That body had the blood drained from it before death; the animal drank his blood."

"What does that mean?"

"It means, young Eric, that we are dealing with a different type of animal. Are you familiar with the story of the lions of Tsavo?"

"Not really, just what Douglas said."

"They were man-eaters that ate a hundred and forty

people. They too drank the blood of their victims. They enjoyed it, as I think this animal enjoys it. If it is the same phenomena, these animals are killing for pleasure, not food."

They hiked back to the jeeps. Thomas spoke with Douglas. Sandra and Will were playing cards in one of the jeeps and the tracker was at the edge of the brush. The man was squatting and in full concentration, staring into the tall grass unblinkingly; his muscles tense and his rifle slung over his shoulder.

The man didn't move when Eric approached.

Eric looked into the grass from behind him. It was longer than he'd seen, about chest high and a dull green-brown. The wind was whipping it back and forth, and it had an eerie voice-like quality from its motion.

The man slowly raised one hand up to his rifle and began to bring it down. He froze mid-motion a few seconds and then continued. Before it was to his chest, Eric heard the grass split apart and a warm spatter of blood hit his face, blinding him, as a shot rang in his ears. Something rammed him. It felt like he was hit by a boulder. It knocked him off his feet as the tracker screamed and was pulled into the brush. The world spun and suddenly Eric was staring at the blue sky from his back. Dizzy and tasting blood in his mouth.

The screams died down but Eric couldn't hear anything. He didn't hear Sandra and Will standing over him and yelling or Thomas and Douglas running into the brush with their rifles. He didn't hear the screams of the children as they ran for protection in their homes or the laughter that echoed through the warm air.

20

Eric floated from a mound of grass to a cloud that sat next to him. The cloud moved purposefully, turning at an angle to fit perfectly between him and the grass. He moved toward the sky and the sun was bright on his face.

"Son?"

Eric was in the backseat of a car. In the passenger seat was Jeff, staring at the road before them. His father was driving and turned back to Eric. "Son?"

"Yeah?"

"You have to make sure there's no water in your shoes. You can't get trench-foot. Wear your boots without socks and stop every hour and dry your feet. It worked when you were in Vietnam. Your grandpa saw you there."

"I will."

"There's the dam."

A large dam sat in the middle of the road, water leaking from millions of little crevices.

"Looks like it's going to burst," his father said.

"Yeah," Eric said. He looked at Jeff. On his head was a

clear bowl of water with a scorpion floating inside.

"Son?"

"Yeah."

"We needed to take a detour."

"Yeah."

Eric felt a sharp pain in his head and it spread over his face, down his neck, over his chest and legs to his feet.

He woke in a cold sweat, Jalani sitting by his cot, applying a wet rag to the wound on his head. The side of his face ached and he felt the stickiness of dried blood on his neck.

"Don't get up," Jalani said. "Dr. Said gave you some antibiotics. You'll be fine, it's just a scratch."

Eric thought back and remembered motion and warmth and pain. He couldn't slow the image down enough to see anything more than a blur.

"Where's the tracker?" Eric said.

"Gone."

Eric reached up and touched his head. "What happened?"

Jalani hesitated. "You were... you were bit, Eric."

Eric saw a flash in his mind's eye. The red and brown of a tongue, and the sharp angles of yellowed teeth scraping his face.

Within a couple of hours, Jalani helped Eric move to one of the jeeps. Will sat next to him. Douglas, Jalani and Thomas were out scouring the neighboring areas with some of the men from the village. Sandra was sitting with the children playing games and calming their nerves. It was still hot and the breeze had died down. The sun was relentless. Will poured sunscreen over himself and applied a few dabs to Eric's nose and neck.

"I've never seen anything move so fast," Eric finally

said.

"What'd you see?"

"I felt blood hit my face and then a streak of fur. Some yellow teeth."

"Nothing else?"

"No."

"Well, I think we should be heading back. This is too dangerous for us."

Thomas eventually appeared out of the brush and approached the jeep. The skin on his hands and knees was cut, and sweat glistened on his neck and face.

"Anything?" Will said.

"Afraid not. It made off with the body as well, damn thing. Must be strong as an ox. I think it might've been a tiger if not for the laughter."

Will said, "If you have anything personal of the tracker, I'd like to perform a service before we left."

"Left?" Thomas said in amazement. "Why would we do that?"

"Are you kidding me? This thing is dangerous. This isn't some safari anymore."

"It never was. You were told it was a hunting trip, were you not?" Thomas's face softened as he saw he was only escalating things. "Look, you're a religious man, Will. You value life as much or more than anyone here. These people are dying every night. Children, women, doesn't matter to the hyenas. They tear their skin off while they're still alive and drink their blood before they eat them. Without bribes, the government authorities don't give a damn. Hiring me was just an act to seem like they're doing something about this. How can we just leave these people as they are without helping?"

Will took a deep breath and glanced at Eric. "Fine, I'll

stay. But Sandra and Eric have to go back."

"No," Eric said.

"What?" Will said incredulously. "Eric, that thing could've killed you."

"That *thing* killed my father. I'm not leaving."

"I'm not leaving either," Sandra said, walking up and standing next to Thomas.

"Sands—"

"No, Will. There's children dying here. Thomas says he can kill it and I believe him."

"You can stay here in the village if you like," Thomas said. "We'll have to go farther out in the plains to hunt them. Some of us will have to stay here, with the women and children."

Will grew angry as he realized Thomas was goading him. "No," he said, "I'll come."

"Good. I think it only fair that Eric comes as well. I'll have Jalani and Douglas stay here with Sandra. They'll be safe enough if they stay in good numbers in the village. Hyenas hunt in clans but they have a matriarch. If we kill the matriarch, the clan will disburse. We won't be long. It's just one animal we need to kill."

"Fine," Will said.

"Why can't we just stay here and wait for it?" Eric said.

"We'll need to be out in the open so we can draw them away from the village."

"Draw them away with what?" Will said.

"With us," Thomas said with a grin.

The first jeep was packed with gasoline, food, and water; enough for three people to last five days. Will said good-bye to Sandra and they hugged. Douglas handed Thomas a couple bottles of whiskey and they took a drink together before Thomas climbed into the jeep.

"I have something for you," Jalani said before Eric got into the backseat of the jeep. She pulled a chrome handgun from a holster around her waist and handed it to him. "Keep this with you. The rifles are only good at long range, not close."

"Thanks," Eric said as he took it with both hands. He'd never held a gun before but didn't want to show it. He tucked it into his waistband, enjoying the weight of it against him. Jalani stood watching him but not saying anything.

Namdi and some of the villagers had gathered around and they waved goodbye as the jeep started along its path. Sandra stood watching a while and then turned away into the crowd. Only Jalani watched until they were out of sight.

21

They followed a path around the brush and took up the trail of blood and broken stems of grass where the tracker's body had been dragged. They drove a few minutes before Thomas stopped and turned the engine off.

"What's wrong?" Will said.

"The trail's stopped." He looked around in all directions. "And I don't see a... wait." Sticking out of the brush was the bloodied stump of a human foot. Thomas jumped out of the jeep and went to look at it. He bent down and saw that it was severed from the ankle. Going into the brush a little farther, he saw the remains of the tracker. He glanced around and then climbed back into the jeep, started the engine, and took off slowly.

"Eric, start pouring out the kill, would you?"

In the back of the jeep was an icebox filled with the entrails and blood of a recently slaughtered lamb. Eric's job was to scoop out handfuls of the guts and blood with a cup and throw them on the ground every five or ten minutes to attract the animals and have them follow the jeep.

"So you think it's only one clan?" Will asked.

"Possibly, but also possibly just one rogue hyena."

"How could one hyena kill this many people?"

"One large matriarch can eat thirty-five pounds of meat in a single sitting. She could go through two people a week rather easily."

"But I mean... I can't believe it would just be one of them."

"It would make sense that one injured or ill matriarch would be responsible. Hyenas don't consider us prey under normal circumstances, so an entire clan stalking us would be completely unique. Besides, we would have seen or heard if there was a clan around. They hunt in packs. This, I think, is a lone matriarch. Probably ousted from a clan or has had her clan killed. Poachers come here and kill the hyenas for their teeth. They grind them up and sell them as magical cures for everything from cancer to heart attacks."

"You said she drinks blood," Eric said.

"Yes, that is unusual. Only a few man-eaters I know of have done that, and they've mostly been lions. They lick the skin off with their tongues and then drink, but hyenas don't have the sandpaper tongues of lions. They would have to tear the skin off and quickly drink it. It's rare, but it's happened before."

They drove under the scorching sun and stopped to rest and refuel in the shade of a large gray rock formation. A herd of small deer was grazing out in front of them and they could see the gray clouds of an oncoming storm in the distance. Will sat in the jeep while Thomas sat on the rocks and ate fruit. Eric couldn't bring himself to get out of the jeep yet.

"How can you be sure it'll follow us and not just go back to the village?" Will asked.

"I can't," Thomas said with a mouthful of pear. "But I'm betting it will. They can't resist the scent of blood, it'll be far more appealing than the scent of live prey."

"How far out are we going to go?"

"Don't know yet. Far as it takes I suppose. There's a village four or so hours east. We should reach there and back at least."

The conversation was broken by the sound of something in the grass. Low and bassed: the breathing of a large animal.

Will and Thomas glanced at each other and then Thomas darted for his rifle in the jeep. He grabbed it and jumped in front, searching the high grass for any movement.

Will took the other rifle and stood up inside the jeep, looking in the opposite direction of Thomas. The deer had sprinted away and they didn't hear the sound again. Eventually, the plains became silent.

"That sounded close," Will said.

"No more than ten meters," Thomas said, squinting down the sight of his rifle. He lowered it and climbed up onto the hood of the jeep for a better look. "I think, gentlemen... we're being hunted."

22

They drove through the short yellow grass in a broad valley. Wild dogs dotted the landscape, their barking occasionally breaking the monotony of the putting engine and the dirt and pebbles crunching underneath the tires. Eric was only scooping out a cup of entrails every fifteen minutes now as they were running low.

"We're almost out," Eric said.

Thomas stopped the jeep. He got out and looked around, staring up at the clouds that covered the peaks of distant mountains. "There's a storm coming. We'll have to set up camp soon if we can't make it to the village."

"What about this?" Eric said, holding up his bloodied cup.

"I'll take care of that."

He took his rifle and climbed up onto the hood of the jeep. Getting down on one knee, he tucked the rifle snuggly against him and took aim at a young deer in a herd close to them. The air crackled with gunfire and the deer stampeded away, the small one limping a few paces and then collapsing.

They decided to set up camp near the kill, underneath a slim, leafless tree. Two tents were set up, one for Thomas and the other for Eric and Will to share. Twilight had started to descend and the sky was a prism of orange and purple, as if it were being burned by the dwindling rays of the sun.

Will got out a frying pan and began melting butter to cook their meal. Thomas, covered in blood, had cut up the deer and filled two coolers to the brim with blood and entrails. He placed some of the prime cuts of meat next to the fire on a cloth, and Will began cutting it up into bite-sized pieces.

"You know, I have to admit," Will said, "I've never had fresh venison before."

"A bit gamey," Thomas said, "but better than many other meats."

Will cooked the meat with pepper and oil and then put it onto three metal plates. As night came, they ate the meat and washed it down with bottles of water, no one speaking. Eric felt tired and nauseated. He'd seen more blood today than ever in his life, and it sickened him.

Thomas drank whiskey and Will smoked a cigar and stared at the flames as they flickered in darkness. Though the herbivores tended to rest, the plains came alive at night with the sounds of insects and the restless prowling of the predators: chirping and singing and the occasional roar or holler composing a symphony.

Thomas and Will sat staring at the fire, neither speaking. They listened to the night and Thomas finished the bottle of whiskey and threw it on the fire. He took out his pipe, stuffed it full of tobacco, and smoked.

Will smirked. "You know, I don't think I've ever actually seen you in a city, Thomas."

Thomas drank something out of a tin cup. "I try to

The Extinct - A Novel of Prehistoric Terror

stay away from the cities. I came out here for freedom from the nonsense of city life. That can kill you as surely as any of the predators out in the plains." He stared into the fire a while. "You think animals are cruel? They're amateurs compared to us. No merciful God could allow us to be his prime creation."

"You're wrong," Will said with a mouthful of smoke. "There is evil, but there's good too, Thomas."

Thomas threw the contents of the cup into the fire and then lay down and closed his eyes. "I haven't seen that side of it yet."

Eric gasped and sat up in the middle of the night. There was laughter outside.

He climbed out of the tent into darkness and could see glowing embers; remnants of the fire in front of him. The night was moonless and a wind was blowing hard. He could feel the patter of droplets of rain against his face and arms. Thomas was already standing outside his tent, his rifle across his chest.

"Go back to sleep, boy," he said. "I'll keep watch."

Eric climbed back into his tent, where Will was sound asleep. But he was unable even to close his eyes. He took out Jalani's gun and held it tightly until morning, listening for any sounds outside.

Every once in a while, he could hear the distant echo of laughter.

23

Jalani stoked the fire, keeping an eye on the rain-clouds moving in. Sandra sat across from her, and Douglas was already drunk and lying next to the fire, warming himself. Namdi sat on a log sipping tea and watching the ashes drift on the wind and land softly on the dirt.

"Tell me something, Doctor," Douglas said, "that elder said one of the children claims the animal talked to it. I've heard myths that hyenas can imitate human voices. Is it true?"

"I don't know," Namdi said. "As a man of science, I say no. But there was a time when I was traveling by myself through Tsavo. I stopped at night near a large clearing and made a fire and put up a tent. I was speaking on my cell phone and I answered it saying 'this is Dr. Said.' In the night before I went to sleep, I heard a noise in the bush. I came out of the tent and saw the yellow eyes of hyenas in the darkness and heard their laughs. I was getting out my rifle when I heard a voice say, 'this is Dr. Said.'"

"Shit," Douglas said. "What did you do?"

"I got into my jeep and drove away. But, one is more likely to be frightened when alone. It was probably a growl that I misheard because I was scared."

They listened to the crash of thunder behind them and could hear the rainfall not more than a mile away. The air now smelled of wet dirt and had a dampness to it.

"You know, Thomas has never told me how he met you," Sandra said to Jalani, probably wanting to change the subject.

"We met in Kigali."

"Rwanda?" Douglas said. "When was this?"

"During the civil war."

"You were there during the war?" Douglas said.

"Yes," Jalani said, obviously uncomfortable.

"Well?" Douglas said. "What happened? How'd you meet?"

"Thomas saved my life. I have stayed with him since then."

"What was it like in the war?" Sandra asked.

"I didn't know what people were until I saw that war. Then, I knew. When Thomas found me, I was being rounded up. I was told I would be forced to leave the country, but I found out from someone else they were just going to kill me. Ten of us and I decided to run. I was only eleven. I was half a kilometer away before one of their trucks came and they shot me in the leg.

"Thomas was near there for some reason. I don't know why. He shot one of the men as the man put a gun to my head. The other men were cowards, they ran." She looked skyward. "It was the worst place in the world. There were hundreds of children without arms or legs that had been cut off. Women were raped in the streets. People were burned in large fires and when they tried to climb out, men would push them back in. I've never seen Thomas cry except while we were there. I don't know if that place has left him."

Slowly, droplets of salty rain fell and the fire began to die down. Douglas looked up to the sky, feeling the water against his face. "I hope they're all right."

"They're fine," Jalani said. "I think we should get to sleep. Tomorrow, we should build some traps."

"How long do you think we should give them before going out to look for them?" Douglas said.

"They have enough food for five days. Then we'll go look for them."

Douglas looked out over the storm clouds, a swirling mass of gray and black, the occasional lightning bolt brightening the sky and thunder booming through the air a few seconds later. "I hope it won't come to that, my friend."

24

The morning was already hot by the time Eric lumbered out of his sleeping bag. His head throbbed and he still had the taste of whiskey in his mouth.

As he climbed out of the tent, he saw Will making eggs over a low fire. The air still had the smell of fresh rain but everything was drying quickly. Eric wondered how this place managed to get enough water when it evaporated the next morning.

"Rough night?" Will said.

"I guess."

"I felt you get up. What happened?"

"The hyena was close. Where's Thomas?"

"Walking around. You want eggs?"

"No, thanks. We got any juice?"

"In the cooler in the jeep."

The herd of deer he'd seen yesterday was gone and they were alone for miles around. Except of course for the birds and insects. They were always there, always just on the edge of his vision. Eventually it got so he'd get used to seeing something flapping out of the corner of his eye, and he learned to ignore it.

Eric went into the brush and urinated before getting a bottle of orange juice out of the cooler and taking a long swig. Glancing around, he couldn't see Thomas. Then he saw a tan wide-brimmed hat sticking up out of the grass and he made his way down to it.

Thomas was crouching, examining some tracks on the ground, lost in thought. His rifle was propped next to him, his hand caressing it.

"What'd you find?" Eric asked.

"Tracks. But not like I've seen before. Look at this, look how deep these are. Deeper than a male lion's." Thomas glanced up and around them. "This may be the kill of a lifetime."

They walked back to the camp to see Will finishing off some eggs and watching a flock of birds maneuver in the sky, twisting and falling close to the ground and then swinging up again in unison.

"Pack up, Will," Thomas said. "I don't want to lose her."

Soon they were traveling again and the scent of the guts Eric was scooping out was making him nauseated. It seemed to him they were moving too far away from everyone else. Thomas had said the village was east, but they were heading north. He wasn't sure if there were any other villages north, but the landscape was getting sparser and he was seeing more predators. He'd already spotted a leopard in a tree staring down at them and heard the roar of a tiger somewhere in the brush.

Will called Sandra on his cell phone but couldn't get any service. He tried a few times and finally turned the phone off and stuffed it into his backpack.

The day went on as slowly as Eric could've imagined

it going. He had to coat the back of his neck with sunscreen and continuously drink water, though that was running a bit low and he had to slow down.

Thomas stopped the jeep to rest in the afternoon near a large grassy hill. Eric could see a few animals at the top of the hill but couldn't make out what they were. He sat down on a rock and was amazed at how tired he was. The sun could drain your energy as much as movement could.

"I wonder where she is?" Will said, gazing into the vast expanse of grass before him.

"Who knows?" Thomas said. "Never did understand them."

"You know, a lot of researchers say they're intelligent. More intelligent than apes, I've heard."

"I don't believe it. I think they're random and that can get mistaken for intelligence."

"It's killed a lot of people and gotten away with it."

Thomas scoffed. "A cow could kill a lot of people if it wanted to and they're dumb as rocks. It's just an animal, it doesn't know anything."

When they began driving again, it was already late in the afternoon. They hadn't seen anything of the hyena, not even tracks.

"What if she's gone back to the others?" Will asked.

"I don't think she has," Thomas said.

"Why?"

"She couldn't get back this fast. They can run far— their hearts are twice the size of a lion's even though they're smaller—but they can't run fast without resting. No, she's still out here."

"But what if—"

Thomas slammed the brakes and the jeep came to an abrupt halt, knocking Eric forward into the back of Will's seat. Thomas held up his hand for silence. He turned off the engine and stared into a patch of long green grass.

"What is it?" Will whispered.

"She's here."

"How can you tell?"

Thomas pointed to an area just next to a tree. In the grass, barely visible, was the back of something in motion. The fur was a gray color and spotted black. Every once in a while, it would poke up a few inches and then back down into the grass.

"Hand me my rifle, Eric," Thomas whispered.

Eric, moving slowly, took the rifle and slipped it in between the seats. Thomas took it and calmly stepped out of the jeep and began to take aim.

As his rifle came up, the beast ducked down and was gone. Thomas made his way to the front of the jeep and then climbed on the hood. There was nothing. As if it had never been there. He fired a shot in the air, startling the other two men. He then took aim into the grass and fired three consecutive shots, the casings clinking as they hit the metal of the jeep on the way to the ground.

After a few moments, Thomas hopped down. "Get your rifles and come with me. We'll try and flush her out of the grass."

When everyone was out of the jeep, Thomas motioned for the other two to go around to the south end of the patch of grass and he would go to the north. Will, Eric behind him, stepped quietly, keeping his eye on the grass. The only sounds he could hear were his own breathing and the beating of his pulse in his ears.

Will nodded to Eric before they went into the thicket of grass. It was slick from last night's rain and made a crunching noise when split apart to allow them through.

They moved cautiously, each step sending a wave of adrenaline through their bodies.

Eric felt something hit his chest and he jumped. He brought his rifle up and saw the birds they'd startled taking off. Relief washed over him. But before he had a chance to relax, what sounded like an explosion rang through the air.

"The jeep," Will said.

They ran out of the grass and down the dirt trail to the jeep. Thomas joined them a second later. The jeep was tilted to one side, both tires on the left completely flat. Thomas examined them; there were large holes on the outside of the rubber, pierced all the way through the tube.

"She knew," Will said. "She knew to draw us away and then attack the jeep."

Thomas looked at him, surprise flashing across his face before disappearing. "She doesn't know anything," he said.

25

"What're we gonna do?" Will said.

"We wouldn't get ten meters on just a rim," Thomas said. "We'll have to walk."

"It'll take us days."

"A Marathi village is only three or four hours walk from here. Gather only what you need."

Driving over the Andhra Pradeshn ground and walking over it were two completely different experiences. Eric found his feet sinking into the soft dirt and he'd have to make an effort to keep an even stride.

They walked for hours, stopping every thirty or forty minutes for some rest in the shade of a large tree or boulder. Water was low; only four bottles left since many had been crushed and spilled during the attack on the jeep. Food wasn't as much of a problem as the intense heat could ward off appetite.

"Do you think she's following us now?" Eric asked.

"I don't know," Thomas said, not turning around.

"Have you killed hyenas before?"

"Plenty. When I was your age, there wasn't an animal

safe from me."

"Why?" Will said. "Why is it you take such pleasure in killing?"

Thomas stopped and turned around. "I've seen hyenas eat a person from very close, Will, closer than you are to me now. You wouldn't be saying that if you'd seen them. The way their bloody faces laughed as they tore—" Thomas hesitated, his face flushed with anger. "Regardless," he said, regaining his calm. "You'd have to see it."

The sun began going down, coloring the sky blue-black as stars began to shimmer. The moon was full and any storm clouds that had been there before had moved on.

Eric could see the outline of the Marathi village in the distance, but as darkness fell, it seemed as if it were as far as the moon. The sounds of animals in the night were like an actual, physical, presence, as if the air itself had been turned to roars and growls. It circled them, enveloped them, and seemed to close off the rest of the world as they slowly began their ascent up a hill that led to the village.

A roar shattered the steady noise of the plains. It was loud and echoed through the valley. The group stopped to listen, Eric gripping his rifle tightly in his hands. It was silent for a minute afterward, but slowly the other animals began their cacophony again, and the valley returned to normal.

"I've never heard an animal make a sound like that," Will said. He looked to Thomas but he was gazing into the dark, not paying attention.

The hill was bare except for short green grass and had no places for large predators to hide. Still, Eric kept his rifle ready, the thought of the tracker's death fresh in his mind.

"Keep moving," Thomas said. "She has to attack from the base and charge. We'll have an excellent shot at her from higher ground."

They kept walking, each step growing more difficult as the hill grew steeper. But the moon was bright and provided enough illumination to light their surroundings. Thomas had gotten far ahead of the other two and was surveying the land in front of them. He wasn't entirely sure this hyena wasn't part of a clan, and hyenas were extremely clever hunters when together.

"We're here," Thomas bellowed.

A hundred yards out lay a small clearing in front of a forest and Eric could see that they were on top of a flat plateau. Lush, tall, grass covered the ground. Brown conical huts were built in a line along the edge of the forest and a few fires were lit here and there. Eric could hear, and smell, masses of cattle herded next to the village.

As they approached, he could see people huddled around the fires. They wore simple cloth wrapped around their bodies and jewelry made of gems and wood. Their faces appeared hard at first and the males grabbed various weapons and began to walk out to meet the interlopers, but one of them recognized Thomas and smiled, giving a command to the others who dispersed.

"Namaste," Thomas yelled out.

"Namaste!" the man said. He wrapped his hand tightly around Thomas's forearm in greeting, as Thomas did the same.

They spoke for a few moments, the man occasionally glancing at Eric and Will. He eventually nodded and waved for them to follow.

"We can stay the night," Thomas said.

"I should call Sandra and have her send someone to pick us up."

"No," Thomas said sternly. "Not until it's dead."

"You can't be serious?"

"We'll have another jeep sent out soon enough, but we can handle this ourselves. Don't call them yet."

"I'll call whoever I damn well please. You know, I think you're losing your mind, Thomas, dragging two people with no experience in hunting to chase this thing. Why didn't you ask Jalani to go with you?"

"You're not calling them," Thomas said softly.

Will took out his cell phone. Before he'd pressed even one number, Thomas grabbed it from him and threw it far down the hill.

"Are you insane!" Will yelled. He grabbed Thomas by the collar and pushed him backward.

Thomas slipped to the side, quickly loosening Will's grasp, and tripped him. Will fell hard as a cloud of dirt was kicked up around him.

"Don't do that again," Thomas said. He glanced at Eric. "Come on, boy, you'll like these people."

Eric helped Will up as Thomas walked away.

"I'm going to get my phone," Will said.

"Not now," Eric said. "We'll get it in the morning."

Will watched Thomas. "He's going to get us killed, Eric," he said somberly.

He pulled away and followed Thomas.

26

They sat around a fire as a villager told stories. He told them in a way Eric had never heard before, using his whole body to weave the tale as children sat at his feet, enthralled. Eric couldn't understand what the story was about, but he knew a storm was involved from the blowing sounds and the wave-like motions of the man's hands. Thomas sat next to the man who had greeted him, talking and drinking. Will was caught up in the man's storytelling as well.

"It's amazing how entertaining this really is," Will said. "I wish I knew what he was saying."

Eric nodded absently.

"What's wrong? Will asked.

"I miss home I guess. And I'm out in the middle of the jungle chasing an animal that almost killed me."

"God puts us where he needs us."

Eric scoffed. "Does everything have to be about God?"

"You know, there's a parable I'm really fond of. A man dies and goes to heaven and he's standing before St. Peter and Peter has his whole life written for him as footsteps on a beach. There's two sets of footprints at the early stages of the man's life and St. Peter explains that that's because God was always with him. Then, in the more troubled times of the man's life, there's only one set of footprints. The man says 'Why did God abandon me when I needed him most?' and St. Peter says 'No, that's when he carried you.'"

Will put his arm around Eric's shoulders. "Tomorrow'll be better, Eric, it always is."

27

The night wore on and Eric grew tired. The villager's stories had ended and the children were put to bed, the women with them. The men sat around now and ate salted chicken and drank a fermented drink out of a communal bowl.

There was a commotion from something coming up the hill and the men jumped up, some grabbing their weapons. Soon, the dim glow of torches could be seen. Eric made out a group of people hiking up toward the village.

It was a group of about five men with a woman walking behind them. As they approached, they were greeted with cheers and what sounded like congratulatory words. When they were close enough that Eric could see them in the light of the fire, he saw that the woman was bound with rope and being pulled by the men.

"What's going on?" Eric said.

"I don't know," Will said, looking over to Thomas. "What is this?"

"Leave it."

The men rose from beside the fire and encircled the

woman, who was cowering and trembling with fear. The men began to grope her, feeling her breasts and buttocks and tearing at her clothes.

"What the hell is this, Thomas?" Will said.

"I said leave it."

One of the men picked the woman up, holding her up in the air and laughing. He tossed her back to the ground and she landed with a thud on her back and began to cry.

Will jumped forward and Thomas quickly stood and got in his way.

"It's none of our business, Will."

"What're they gonna do with her?" Will said.

Thomas didn't respond. He just looked to the woman and then back to Will.

Will said loudly, "What are they gonna do with her, Thomas?"

Thomas gazed in his eyes, unwavering. He had the innate ability to look through somebody as if they just weren't there. "They're going to take her in that hut and rape her. They may or may not kill her when they're through."

Eric could tell Will was barely able to hold in his anger. "Why?"

"She's a capture from a rival tribe. It's the way of things out here. The authorities leave it alone, and so will we."

"The hell we will. We'll stop them."

"We'll do no such thing. Sit down, eat your food, and drink your drink. This has nothing to do with you."

The woman fought as they dragged her into one of the huts, the men laughing.

"Stop them, Thomas," Will said frantically. "Stop them now!"

"I can't."

"In the name of God, stop them!" He tried to push his way past, but Thomas wrapped his arms around him and held on with an iron grip.

"If you interfere, they will kill us. We're their guests."

"Damn you!" Will yelled, pulling away. Thomas swept his feet out from under him and Will landed on his back.

Thomas sat on his legs and pinned his arms to his chest. "I won't let you kill us over this. Trust me, this is not unjustified. The other tribe has done very similar wrongs to this tribe and no doubt they will want revenge for this. It will go on and on, as it probably has for centuries."

Will fought with all the strength he had, but his frail physique was no match for the surly Thomas. He stopped struggling, closing his eyes and praying instead. As he heard the screams, tears ran down his cheeks.

Soon afterward, the men came out of the hut, some of them wiping bloodied hands on their bellies. Thomas sat back down near the fire as if nothing had happened.

Will rose to his knees and then stood up. "Damn you," he hissed. He stumbled off, heading down the hill. Eric rose to grab him.

"Let him be," Thomas said, not looking up. "He's just drunk. He'll be fine."

Eric looked down the hill until Will was out of sight. He turned back to Thomas, who was busy getting drunk and staring at the flames. Eric came and sat across from him.

"What?" Thomas said.

"I didn't say anything."

"By the way you're staring at me, I can tell you want

to. So, just say it."

"You could've stopped them."

Thomas took a long gulp of the drink and held the bowl in his lap, running his fingers along the edge. "I had a dream the other night. It was of a pond I used to visit with my father when I was young, I think it was called Topps Pond. It was a beautiful place, a small body of water on the top of a mountain near our home, all the plants a bright green around the water's edge. We used to fish there, though, later, I found out there were none there. My father just wanted to spend time with me.

"I had my first exposure to death in that pond. It was an old dog we had. I can't remember his name. He had a toy ball I used to throw around. One day we were at the pond and my father fell asleep in the boat. I threw the dog's toy in the water, thinking he'd swim it back. For whatever reason the dog couldn't swim. I thought he was fine under the water. By the time my father woke up the dog was dead.

"I hated the pond after that. I refused to go, and soon my father stopped asking." Thomas finished off the rest of the drink and threw the empty bowl on the ground. "In my dream, I was at that pond again as a child. I was staring into the water and I was so full of hate. But I was looking at my reflection, and there was no hate looking back at me... the pond just didn't care." Thomas stared off into the distance, unblinking. He finally took a deep breath and looked at Eric, his eyes softening. "Anyway, I've waxed philosophical long enough. I'm drunk and going to bed." He rose and stumbled off into the night.

Eric stared into the flames. One of the tribe, a male who had raped the woman, walked to him and took the empty bowl off the ground. He went to a large vat across the village and filled it up again. He brought the bowl over to Eric and, smiling, offered it to him. Eric took the bowl and the man seemed pleased.

The man still had smears of blood over his skin from the woman, but it didn't seem to bother him. For the first time Eric realized these people were not like him. Not just in appearance or culture, but in soul, too. They were part of the landscape, part of the jungle itself.

He tilted the bowl and spilled out the drink onto the dirt, watching as drops splashed into the fire. The body of the woman was brought out by two men and dragged into the forest. Eric watched the fire a while and then kicked dirt onto the flames, extinguishing it and leaving himself in sullen darkness.

28

The next day came solemnly as the tribe gathered in front of the huts. They were discussing Thomas's request for a few men to take out on the hunt. Thomas stood with them, speaking their tongue perfectly. He nodded and gripped forearms again with one of the men.

Thomas walked to Eric who was sitting on the dirt by the embers of last night's fire. "Sleep well?"

"Where's Will?"

"He didn't return last night."

"What? We gotta go find him," Eric said, jumping up and searching for his boots.

"We will," Thomas said placatingly. "Relax for now. The tribe has agreed to loan us a few of their men today for the hunt."

Eric didn't respond. Thomas sat down in the dirt and took out his pipe.

"You disagree with what I did last night," Thomas said.

"You could've helped the woman. She didn't do anything wrong."

"No, but she would've. Fifteen years from now, that young woman's son would be doing the same thing to one of this tribe. Make no mistake about this place, there's no room to be soft."

Eric stepped past him. "Maybe not for them, but there is for us."

The women and children stared and whispered as Eric made his way through the village and down the hill. He could see the environment clearly now: they were up on an embankment that connected to a larger mountain. Below them was green shrubbery and short grass. Asian elephants in the distance were making their way to the nearest watering hole and he could see the striped black and gold lines of deer sticking out of the landscape like paint on a canvas.

Eric came to the base of the hill and looked back; no one had followed him. He took out his handgun and kept it low.

"Will," he shouted. "Will!"

He hiked past the shrubbery to a nearby rock formation. "Will!"

As he made his way around the conical formation, he got a better view of the tops of the lower boulders. Will was sprawled on one of them, his shirt pulled up over his face to keep out the sunlight.

"Will!" Eric shouted as he jogged over. "You okay?"

Will belched and tasted whatever fermented drink he'd been served last night. He removed the shirt and squinted as his eyes adjusted to the daylight. "I couldn't find my phone."

"I'll help you find it now and then we'll get outta here."

"You want to leave?"

"Yeah, I don't want to be here anymore. Let's get someone to pick us up and go back to Kavali."

Will, groggy and still half-drunk, nodded and started to get up. Eric helped him to his feet.

"Where's Thomas?" Will asked.

"He's got some of the tribe to help him hunt."

They made their way off the boulder and began searching the hill. It was soon apparent how difficult finding the phone was going to be. The dirt had been kicked up from the wind, and the grass was long enough to hide something as small as a cell phone. As they searched, they saw Thomas lead a group of four men down past them. He looked at them and smiled wryly.

"Keep looking, Eric," Will said, averting his eyes from Thomas'.

They searched for a long time, taking only a quick rest to drink water and take care of toiletries behind some trees. In the end, the task was impossible. And even if they did find the phone it'd been thrown far and might not be working.

"Let's stop," Will said, his shirt sticking to him with sweat. "I don't think we're gonna find it."

"Maybe we can walk to a town?"

Will looked out over the brush, squinted, and rubbed at the burnt skin on his nose. "Without much food or water I don't know how far we'd get. It could be days on foot. And that thing's still out there. But I don't think I can stay here anymore, not with these people. I'm going, but don't feel like you have to come."

"No, I'm coming."

Will wiped the sweat off his brow with the back of his hand. "All right, get my rifle and as much food and water as you can carry."

Eric ran up the hill and gathered what Will had asked. The tribe didn't seem to notice him now. They were busy in their day-to-day activities and didn't have time to worry about an outsider. He took what he could and ran back down the hill. Will was staring in the distance.

"I think if we go west we should get there in about two days on foot."

They left the village then and Eric looked around for Thomas, but didn't see him. Within a short time, he couldn't see the village anymore.

They walked through the thicket of bushes, past the herd of elephants, and in less than an hour were out far enough that the hill itself was an indistinct blur in the distance.

"You ever been to Thailand?" Will asked.

"No."

"This place reminds me of Thailand. Parts of it are beautiful and other parts not so much. I was in the jungle once and it was raining really hard and the sun came up from behind some clouds but the rain didn't let up. It looked like the whole sky was one giant rainbow. And our guide got bit by this snake that night in his tent. He didn't make it. Beauty and death I guess."

The air was thick with heat. Eric took off his shirt and rolled up his pant legs. By the afternoon, he was burned a light pink and the skin on the back of his neck would sting whenever sweat rolled down from his scalp.

It became clear to him that they were absolutely in the middle of nowhere. There were large mountains to one side of them far off across the plains; instead of ending in peaks they were topped with flat plateaus. On the other side was a vast expanse of short-grassed plains, teaming with life and vegetation. Heat waves were streaming from the ground as they went past a plethora of trees huddled together.

"Stop," Will said. He stood perfectly still, listening. His eyes were unblinking and they grew wider as he realized what he was hearing.

He walked slowly near the trees and ducked low in the grass. He motioned for Eric to come down next to him.

"What is—" Eric stopped mid-sentence when he saw what Will was looking at. In front of them, not more than twenty yards, was a tiger feeding on the carcass of a deer.

The massive animal roared and it sent shivers down Eric's spine. He'd never seen anything so inspiring of awe and fear. From this close, he could see its true bulk and the packed muscles contracting in its jaws and legs.

"We'll go around," Will whispered.

Eric followed him two or three hundred meters out from the tiger and they started west again. The heat was getting to the point of being unbearable and Eric was starting to feel lightheaded. In this weakened, dizzy state, the Andhra Pradeshn landscape seemed as alien to him as observing another planet. Every rock and tree and blade of grass looked like it didn't belong in the same world as he did.

"Where'd you meet Sandra?" Eric said, trying to make conversation to get his mind off what he was feeling.

"Boston. Her sister was a friend of mine and she introduced us," Will said, happy to talk about his wife. The very thought of her put a smile on his face. "Eric, there's nothing quite like falling in love. It affects everything else. It's almost indescribable; you just have to go through it to see how far into your life it can reach."

They ended the conversation at that, speaking taking

up too much effort at this point.

Evening came before long and the sky lit up crimson, the sun a yellow orb in an ocean of red. Though tired and with a growing worry of the coming darkness, they couldn't help but stop for a while and admire the view.

"Are you tired enough for sleep?" Will asked.

"Definitely."

"Let's do two hours each and the other person keep watch."

Eric put his shirt back on and lay down in front of a large tree. Will sat next to him, his rifle across his lap. Eric closed his eyes and could hear the chirping of birds over his breathing as he fell into a dreamless sleep.

29

Eric awoke to Will's nudging. It was dark now, and a crescent moon hung in the sky. The air was warm and had wafts of dust in it from a strong wind. Eric grudgingly rose and saw Will gazing into the valley before them. A small fire was built in front of him but provided little light or warmth.

"What is it?" Eric said.

Will's gaze was unmoving, his voice steady. "It's here."

Eric watched the darkness, the trill chirps of thousands of crickets aggravating him and increasing his fear. There was nothing he could see and he wondered if Will was just too fatigued. But gradually, as his eyes adjusted, he could see two small glowing lights. They were slits of red, and they were circling them. The lights stopped, fixated, and began a silent approach.

"Run," Will said.

Eric ran. The wind was loud in his ears but he could still make out the crunching of tall weeds and grass behind them. He looked back only to see the slits of red closing in.

"Up there!" Will shouted.

There were large boulders piled atop one another and Eric sprinted for them. He leapt onto the first and grabbed Will's hand and helped him up. They climbed on the rough, dry surface of the rock and only stopped when they reached the top. Eric's breathing was labored and his heart felt like it would explode. He took out his hand-gun and held it in front of him.

"Did you see it?" he said.

"No, just its eyes," Will said, out of breath. "You watch behind us. Shoot for the head if it charges up the rocks."

Only the sound of their breathing filled the awful silence; the crickets had stopped. And, somewhere out in the dark, laughter.

The laughter could've been human. Eric thought it was the type of laugh that an insane person would have, menacing and meaningless. As though threatening someone that wasn't there.

"Why isn't it attacking?" Eric said.

"I don't know."

Will saw the slits of red glowing like embers in the dark. He pointed the rifle, trying to steady his shaking hands. He aimed and pulled the trigger. The eyes disappeared in the night.

"Did you hit it?" Eric asked.

"I don't know, maybe."

"We should run."

"I don't think we'd get very far. At least from here we can see around us."

They sat on the warm stone through the night. By morning, Eric's legs and back were stiff and throbbed with pain. His eyes were blurry from a lack of sleep and he found it difficult to think. The sun rose slowly and ignited the colors of the plains before them. There was nothing surrounding them but the brush.

Will stood up. He made his way down the boulders and out to where he thought he might have hit the animal. Eric climbed down and stood behind him. There was trampled grass and deep paw prints, but no blood.

"Let's get going," Eric said.

"I'm not sure if it was... it."

"Who cares? Let's just get outta here."

They hurried back to their supplies and saw with horror that their food was scattered and mostly eaten. The remaining water bottles had been ripped open and the plastic containers were slowly tumbling in the wind across the valley. They walked off without saying a word.

It had the makings of being another scorching day and Eric feared what it would feel like in a few hours without any water. He surveyed his surroundings in detail and came to the conclusion that none of it looked familiar.

"I don't think we're going in the right direction, Will."

"Me neither. But there's got to be people somewhere around here."

"We could go back to the village."

Will looked around. "I have no idea which direction that is. Do you?"

"No."

"We're lost, Eric. Best thing to do when you're lost is just pick a direction and keep going."

An uneasy feeling came over Eric, and the thought entered his mind that they were never going to leave this place.

30

It had started pouring rain. The storm came out of nowhere and within a few minutes had drenched them. It was unlike anything Eric had ever seen; as if the sky were bleeding water. It gushed in thick, heavy sheets and stung the skin on his face when it spattered against him. Off in the distance he could see lightning brightening the sky and thunder would crackle a few seconds later. The ground turned to mud. Walking became difficult, but they kept going; stopping only when evening fell.

They approached a large ravine. There was a small stream running across the bottom and the sides were coated in long green weeds. They sat down under a large tree and Will took his boots off. His socks were wet and he stripped them off, revealing white blistered feet.

"Damn it," he said. "Who would've thought you'd have to worry about trench-foot in a hundred and twenty degree weather." He threw his socks over the edge of the ravine, slipping his boots back on over his feet. "Little tactic I picked up from a Vietnam vet," Will said. "You stop every hour and air your feet out... Eric? You okay?"

"Fine. Who'd you know that was in Vietnam?"

"One of the homeless men that came to the church for the free Sunday dinner. A lotta homeless were in that war." He shook his head. "Damn fine waste of good men." Will scooted back underneath a large branch, trying to keep the downpour off his head. "So what was your father like? You never talk about him."

"He was a good man. I don't think he was ever happy but he always treated me good. What about yours?"

"I don't remember my father. My mother said he was in the second World War, but I don't even know if that's true. One of my uncles got drunk one night and told me she had a one night stand and never saw the guy again." Will looked off into the ravine. "Weird feeling, to hate your father though you've never met him." He leaned forward, over the ledge. "Hey, look at this."

Eric looked over into the ravine. Two small balls of fur were bouncing around on a ledge. They were a golden color with black spots; leopards. They couldn't have been more than a few months old.

"Cute little bastards," Will said. "Hope mama doesn't pick up our scent." He lay back and closed his eyes. "Might as well get some sleep if you can."

The rain cleared up as quickly as it had come and the clouds vanished. The sun pounded the earth again and within hours the plains were dry. It was odd how quickly the weather changed out here and it was something Eric was certain he could never get used to. Life was unstable and unpredictable enough without the environment being the same way.

They walked through a particularly thick patch of

grass and came out the other side onto a narrow dirt road. Will looked one way, and then the other.

"It's gotta lead somewhere," Eric said.

"Yeah, but which way?"

The road went on in both directions well past the limits of vision. Eric examined it more carefully. It wasn't a road built intentionally; it was a path that had been beaten down through the grass.

"Why would so many people come through here?"

"Who the hell knows?" Will looked both ways again and then said, "Well, what do you think?"

Laughter behind them.

They both turned and looked into the grass, unable to see anything. There was some movement far off and Will raised his rifle, but didn't fire.

"I'm thinking either one is as good as the other," Will said.

"Yeah," Eric said, not taking his eyes off the grass.

Neither of them could concentrate as they walked, each glancing over their shoulder. Whenever they'd hear the slightest noise they would stop and raise their rifles. They'd wait half a minute before walking again.

They saw something in the distance as they walked. It was a dark speck at first, but as they approached, they saw the square outline of a building. It was made of dark red brick and was about the size of a large house. The front door was open.

They went up some steps to the door and peeked in. It was a reception area. There was garbage strewn all over the floor and a single desk took up half the space in the room. The place looked like it'd just been ransacked. "Hello?" Will yelled. He looked back to Eric and shrugged before walking in.

The air stunk even though the door had been open. A slight breeze was blowing and causing some of the papers to rustle. Eric could see a rotting half-eaten lunch on the desk. Will went to the desk and flipped through some of the papers.

"It's a medical facility," Will said.

"Where is everyone?"

"I don't know." There were some metal drawers against the wall and Will opened each one, examining the contents before closing the drawer and going to the next one. "Some of this stuff's in English." He looked around. "They've got to have a bathroom somewhere, which means they have to have water."

Eric followed Will down a narrow hallway and into the first room. It looked like an office, but there was no furniture; only garbage thrown around everywhere. One of the windows was broken and sunlight reflected off the little pieces of glass on the floor.

They went to the next room. It was a medical examining room. Will found some band-aids and antiseptic in one of the cupboards and he stuffed some into his pockets.

Eric searched the room. There were tongue depressors, thermometers, stethoscopes and even an X-ray machine, but no food or water. They walked out of the room and to the last door at the end of the hallway. Will checked that his rifle was chambered.

The room smelled of feces. They looked in and could see black spatters of blood all over the walls, baked into the paint from the heat. Two bodies were on the floor, a male and female. Stab wounds covered the woman's flesh and her head had a large fracture. The man had been decapitated, his head placed on a desk against the wall. He had lost control of his bowels.

Will said a silent prayer and covered his nose with his shirt to keep out the stench.

Eric had to get out of the room. He leaned against the wall in the hallway and looked out a window on the far side of the reception area. He felt the acid in his throat and couldn't swallow in time to keep the vomit down. What little hydration he had spewed out of him and over the wall.

Will walked out to him and leaned against the opposite wall. "Thuggees," he said. "They have roving gangs all over this valley that do things like this."

"Why? There's nothing here for them to steal."

"Don't think that matters to them." Will stood up straight. "I need your help, Eric, we need to bury them."

Eric had to breathe out of his mouth from the stench. They tore down some curtains and rolled the corpses onto them, dragging them outside and leaving large smears of blood on the floor. A ditch was dug in the soft dirt using the metal drawers from a filing cabinet. They dragged the bodies to the edge of the ditch, rolled them in, then covered them back up with dirt. Will said a prayer.

"I hate this place," Eric said, tears welling up in his eyes. He was beginning to shake. "I hate it."

"Calm down, Eric," he said softly.

"No. This is hell, Will. We're in hell."

Will watched him a moment and said, "Maybe. But we're gonna keep going all the same."

Night came quickly as they sat in the reception room, staring out the windows. Will tried to pass the time by reading some of the medical documents he'd found and cleaning his rifle. Eric sat silently, unmoving. They'd found some candles and had them set up around the room, providing a warm glow in the darkness.

"These people suffered so much," Will said, flipping through some papers. "It seems like everyone was dying of things that could be cured in the States with a prescription."

There was barking outside. Will looked to Eric and dropped the papers. He picked up his rifle and made his way to the door. Eric didn't want to move, but he forced himself up. He went behind Will and stared out into the darkness.

The moon provided some illumination and they could make out the shapes of animals running around in front of the building. They were hyenas, about six or seven of them. They were no bigger than dogs but they struck a fearsome shape in the dark.

They were digging up the corpses. Two of the larger animals were fighting over what looked like a leg. Another one held the woman's corpse by the head and was dragging it up out of the ground.

Eric took out his handgun and fired, the bullet whizzing by Will's ear. He fired again and hit one of the larger hyenas in the leg. The clan, hollering with fear and anger, scattered.

Will grabbed Eric's arm and forced it down. "Don't waste your ammunition. These aren't it. They're too small."

Will shut the front door and sat down against the wall.

As the hours passed, the air grew so humid Eric couldn't breath and it was too uncomfortable to sleep, but he thought he would try anyway.

"We'll leave here in the morning," Will said.

Eric stared out the window at the moon. Outside he could hear barking again, and the sound of something being dragged away. Soon there was just the darkness, and laugher echoing through the valley.

32

Morning came and they began their trek again. As they left the building, they noticed the empty ditch where they'd buried the corpses and the drag marks leading into the nearby brush.

Though it was morning the heat had probably reached into the hundreds, and without water walking was becoming more difficult.

The first thing Eric noticed about severe dehydration was the numbness in his lips. They cracked and stung whenever he licked them. Soon his legs began to feel sore and he couldn't think clearly. After a few hours in the heat, the last of his body's hydration leaked out onto his skin to try to offset the intense heat. His muscles cramped and he realized he wouldn't be able to walk for much longer.

A rustling behind some nearby trees.

Will stopped and lifted his rifle. Eric took a step back and pulled out his gun, holding it low rather than waste the strength to point it. He didn't have the strength to lift his rifle.

There was a patch of gray fur spotted black in the thick shrubbery.

Will pointed his rifle and fired, a swarm of birds leaping from the grass and taking flight. The crackle echoed across the valley.

The fur ducked low and was gone.

"What the hell is it?" Eric said.

Will tried to spit on the ground and it spattered onto his boot. Dust and dirt were constantly swarming with the wind and it gave them a taste like they had been sucking on sand all day. "It's her," he said.

"How do you know?"

"I just know."

Another streak of fur, this time farther away and heading in the opposite direction. Will took aim and fired and the fur ducked low again.

An icy chill went down Eric's back. "Stop," he said.

"What?"

"Don't shoot anymore."

"Why?"

"She's doing it on purpose."

"Doing what?"

"Making us waste our bullets."

Will stared at him a long while and then back out over the grass. The wind had died down and a breeze was rustling through the trees, an invisible hand gently stroking the leaves.

"Let's get moving," Will said solemnly.

Walking soon became torture and Eric had to break down his goals into smaller chunks. Finding civilization was reduced to finding a good road and then walking a hundred feet and then fifty, twenty... and then all he could do to keep his body in motion was to focus on the next step. One step, and then muster strength for one more. He kept his eyes on the tall grass surrounding him, his ears attuned to every sound. But he couldn't help his eyes from falling to his feet, concentrating on each step so as not to fall. If he fell, he wasn't sure he could get back up.

After hours of scorching heat, pain, and blistering skin, they reached a clearing. There was nothing to hide behind, no bushes or trees, and all the life had to be out in the open; each animal sizing up the others. There was a carcass of a deer on the dirt road and Will looked it over as they passed by. There were no signs of it being attacked.

"I think it died of heat," Will said.

They sat down on the dirt road as there was nowhere in sight that provided shade. Will lay flat on his back with his arms and legs wide, trying to cool down. Eric fanned himself with his shirt but the small amount of breeze created was hot and moist so he stopped and just wrapped the shirt around the top of his head to keep the sun off.

In the distance were a series of glimmers, like sunlight reflecting off water or metal. They watched the glimmers get larger for some time before they realized it was people moving toward them.

Will stood up and waved his arms to attract their attention. Eric sat motionless, too fatigued to move. Will found he couldn't wave his arms for long and eventually just sat down, exhausted. The people were moving toward them.

"Let's hope they speak English," Will said.

As the group approached, Eric could see they were two women and probably six or seven men. The glimmers they'd seen was sunlight reflecting off their weapons.

The men carried older rifles. They had the red markings in the center of their foreheads and only a few of the men wore shirts. One of them had a necklace made from some big animal's teeth.

Will stood up, smiling, and nodded hello.

The group watched them with curiosity but Eric didn't detect any fear. He couldn't decide if that was good or bad.

"We need water," Will said. He motioned up to his lips like he held an invisible glass. "Water," he said again. They remained silent. Will wiped at the small amount of sweat that had gathered on his brow and showed it to them before licking it. "Water."

One of the men said something in a harsh, abrupt language and one of the women stepped forward. She took out a little leather pouch and laid it on the ground. Will approached the pouch cautiously and picked it up; the contents swished. He took a sip; warm water.

Will handed the water to Eric and let him drink. He was surprised; he never imagined that water could taste so good. Will laid the pouch on the ground and nodded again. "Thank you," he said. He put his hand on his heart and bowed low. "Namaste."

The group watched them a moment longer and then began moving away. The man that had allowed them water stayed behind.

He patted his hand against his chest. "Tamil'."

"Tamil," Will said. He tapped his fist against his own chest. "Will."

The man nodded. He waited a second and then spoke some words. Seeing that the men didn't understand,

Tamil motioned with his rifle in the universal gesture to follow and began walking away.

Will looked around. "I wasn't sure if bushmen like this existed in India. Looks like I don't really know anything about this place. My vote is to follow them unless you got a better plan."

Eric forced himself up. "No. Let's go."

33

Eric strolled next to Will as they followed the group. They didn't appear like the other tribe. They didn't speak to each other, or sing, or look around at their surroundings. They were focused and serious. So much so that it didn't seem like they noticed the intense heat.

The women were in the center of an oval with the men taking up the spaces outside. Eric noticed they had feet like leather, thick skin with thin sandals.

They navigated through the plains well. It was amazing that they knew where they were going at all, considering they barely glanced up from the ground. They seemed to have an innate sense of where they were.

"What tribe are they?" Eric whispered.

"I don't know. I have a book on the different indigenous people and I don't remember seeing a group like this other than gypsies. There is a *Chenchu* tribe out here that still hunts for subsistence and it could be them."

They walked until dusk and then stopped on a patch of lush green grass. The group sat down in a circle and Eric and Will sat on the outside. The group made a space and Tamil motioned for them to sit. They moved up and sat next to him.

Some of the women took out a black liquid from little leather pouches and began applying it to the foreheads of the men, over the red markings. The men sat cross-legged and closed their eyes. They began humming at first, a low rhythmic sound varying in pitch from high to low. They kept it up a few minutes then stood and began clapping their hands in rhythm. One of them let out a shout and a few others followed.

One of the men walked to the center of the circle and began speaking, describing a story with animated movements and facial expressions.

Each man took their turn in the center of the circle as the sun went down. They passed around a small bottle, each taking a sip before giving it to the man next to them. The climax of the ritual was prolonged yelling, nearly to the point of going hoarse. The women rose and walked next to them, kissing each one on both cheeks before stepping away and sitting back down.

The men turned and began a slow jog to the north. Tamil motioned for them to follow again. They rose slowly and tried to keep pace.

"I can't run," Eric said.

"Just walk as fast as you can."

The men galloped far ahead of Eric and Will, but because the land was so bare, they never lost sight of each other. Eventually they came across a herd of deer and the men stopped and ducked low. By the time Eric and Will had caught up, two of them were already crawling on their bellies toward the animals, rifles held tightly in their hands.

Tamil held his hand flat in the air with his palm facing down and lowered it until it touched the ground. The rest of the men silently got to their bellies and Eric and Will followed.

The deer didn't seem agitated though it'd be hard for Eric to tell. They grazed and let their young wander around without adults near them. A couple were neighing and butting their necks against each other, nipping at their bodies with dull teeth. Tamil pointed to one of them and the men rose and began going in that direction.

"Should we stay here?" Eric said.

"He didn't ask us to follow. I think they only wanted us to come so we would be away from the women."

The two men who had gone off on their own crawled in the opposite direction of the rest of the group. Eric could see that they were heading toward a young doe that was grazing by itself. The rest of the group slowly made their way across to the fighting males. The males were too distracted to notice the approaching hunters.

The two lone hunters slowly rose to their knees, their rifles taking aim. They looked over to the rest of the group and waited until they had done the same.

It seemed almost in unison when they fired. A high pitched squeal rang through the air as panic gripped the deer. The doe was wounded but was still running faster than the men who'd begun chasing it. One of the group had shot a full-size buck, but the wound was superficial and it was getting away.

Eric watched as the doe became sluggish. It seemed disoriented and began running in a wide circle. The men were walking casually a few dozen yards behind it now. The doe neighed and shook its head vigorously as it spun around, bucking and kicking. It stopped abruptly, watching the two men, and then fell to the ground with a loud squeal. The men approached and one took out a long blade. He grabbed the animal by the head and slit its throat. The blade was too dull to do it in one or two motions so he had to saw at the animal's neck until blood poured into the dry earth.

The rest of the men gathered around the dying creature. Tamil brought out a small bowl from a pouch and held it underneath the stream of blood. He brought the bowl to his lips and tilted his head back, guzzling with obvious pleasure. He refilled the bowl and passed it around to the other men.

They drank their fill until the animal died. Tamil closed his eyes and began a chant that Eric thought sounded like a prayer. The men appeared serene as they joined in, their faces calm with bloodstained lips. Tamil began rocking back and forth as if in a trance. He opened his eyes suddenly and was looking directly at Eric. His eyes were distant and unwavering, like two gems set in his skull. He turned around as the other men chanted louder and slit the creature's belly, thrusting the bowl into the wound and filling it once more with dark blood. He rose and walked over to Eric and Will.

Tamil offered up the bowl to Will first. Will looked to Eric and then to the bowl. The blood wasn't as thin as it was right after the kill. It was syrupy and almost a dark purple. Will took the bowl with both hands, and put it to his lips. He lowered it after a second and handed it to Tamil.

It was Eric's turn next. He took the blood and looked down into the bowl. He could see his reflection, wavy and indistinct in the light. Bringing the bowl up, he took two deep swallows.

The blood was warm, almost hot. It tasted like rancid meat and had a thick, slimy texture. It had already congealed a bit and he had to chew the last portion and swallow.

Eric tried to hand the bowl back to Tamil as vomit spewed forth and over his shirt. He kneeled down and started puking bile and deer blood. The smell of the concoction made him doubly sick and he dry-heaved; his stomach empty.

Will's eyes widened and his hand reached for the rifle that was slung over his shoulder. He couldn't be sure that such an insult wasn't an executable offense. But Tamil just stared, and eventually his eyes softened. He smiled and began to laugh. His laugh was deep and took over his whole body. Leaning his head back, he exposed small white teeth and a light pink tongue. The other men saw what was happening and they too began to laugh.

"I don't think they find you very manly," Will said.

"How did you drink that?" Eric said, gagging.

"I didn't, I just put it to my lips."

Eric looked at him banefully and then dry-heaved again.

34

The kill was hauled back to a small encampment near a hill. As darkness fully descended, the bushman lit an enormous fire in a pit the women had dug out with their hands. They stabbed sharpened sticks through the meat and cooked it over the pit until it was crisp. Tamil gave their guests the biggest portions of meat.

The food was good, a bit like spicy beef. Eric ate two large slabs quickly and felt sick afterward.

They were kind to the point of being flawed. There was enough meat to go around this time, but Eric had a feeling that even if there wasn't, they still would've given the biggest portions to them.

After the meal, the group sat around in a circle in front of Tamil as he spoke. His speech was peppered with noises and hand motions and the group was fully entertained. Their attention never wavered from him. Not to the bright glowing moon or the shimmering stars blanketing the sky. They seemed to have an ability to focus completely on what they were doing at any particular moment.

Eric watched Tamil with a sense of wonder. The way he moved and spoke reminded him of some ancient shaman, sitting around a cave telling his tribe about the wonders of the world outside.

Just behind Tamil, in Eric's peripheral vision, he saw movement.

It wasn't much at first; just a blurry streak. Then Eric made out a moving shape. It looked like it was moving slowly but as his eyes adjusted he saw that it was traveling from a great distance through the grass and barreling toward them at incredible speed.

"No!" Eric shouted as he jumped to his feet.

Before the tribe could respond, the beast bit down into Tamil. The flesh on his shoulder and back tore as he let out a scream and was dragged back into the night by his arm. It was hard to make out much more than the head of the creature, but it was massive. Its eyes glowed a faint red in the darkness. Tamil flew backward into the bush as easily as a leaf being blown by the wind. He was dragged fifty feet in a couple of seconds and disappeared. His screaming didn't stop but slowly dimmed to nothing, like a passing ship in the night sea.

Will was running past the fire and into the bush. He leapt over some thick shrubbery and continued sprinting, the thorny vegetation tearing at his clothes and skin. There was a trail in the dirt where Tamil had been dragged. It went into the tall grass and then stopped near a dark circle. Will bent down and touched the circle; it was wet and had a coppery smell. There was no sign of the man other than one of his small leather pouches. Will picked it up.

Eric stood next to him as he searched for paw prints to follow but could find none. Before long, they realized it was hopeless and began walking back.

A thought struck Eric as he made his way back to the fire; the tribesman hadn't helped. Some of it was the speed and surprise of the attack, but even after that they hadn't done anything. He approached them now and they still sat in the same positions, looks of terror across their faces. The only ones who had moved were the women who had encircled one of their younger members who was weeping. Perhaps Tamil's wife, Eric thought. He handed her the small pouch.

"We need to leave," Will said.

"Now?"

"We're a danger to these people, Eric."

"How? That thing could've attacked—"

"That animal's following us. These people aren't safe while we're with them. They're clearly brave but none of them ran after that thing. They're either scared to death of it or think it's some deity or something. Either way, we need to get outta here."

35

Eric and Will walked through the night and well into the next day. They'd made their way past a large valley, over a small hill, and into another valley.

Quick moving gazelles darted around in front of them, the small animals stopping to graze every so often. Roars of the big cats were continually echoing in the distance, and the trumpeting of Asian elephants sometimes followed. There was a river along their path and they rested for what seemed like hours, dousing themselves in the brown water. Will made a fire and they boiled the water in Will's flask before drinking. It was warm and tasted like mud, but they drank two full flasks each before they felt sick and bloated from the dirt that was mixed with it.

Eric took off his shirt and lay in the wet dirt of the riverbank. His head was spinning and he wasn't able to think clearly. His thirst satisfied, he now turned his attention to hunger. "Can we get anything to eat?"

Will sat on the bank. "I saw some berries on a tree, but I can't be sure they're not poisonous. I guess we could try to hunt something."

"What? Like a gazelle?"

"They're fast, but not impossibly fast." He stood up, walking to the river and dousing himself with as much water as he could. He slicked his hair back with his hand and grabbed his rifle. "I'll be back soon."

Eric felt as if he should follow, but he couldn't move. His muscles were so fatigued they had started to spasm and his back had seized up. He covered his eyes with his hands, trying to keep out the blazing sun, but it still slipped through his fingers in a glowing red.

Soon, he was alone with the sun above him, the wet dirt underneath him, and the flowing river in front of him. The rushing waters sounded hypnotic, making him doze off and fall into a dreamless sleep.

A low grumble woke Eric. It sounded like a diesel engine starting in the water. Eric looked up and saw the cracked gray-green scales of an enormous crocodile.

The croc watched him patiently from the water, slowly drifting its tail back and forth as it made its way to the riverbank. Its eyes were sticking out above the surface, but the rest of the animal was submerged.

Eric tried to stand, fighting the resistance of his back and legs. The croc kept a slow pace. Eric was about to turn and run when he heard a loud hiss. Behind him was another croc, though smaller than the one in the river. It had soundlessly come out farther down the bank and crept behind him. It was motionless except for its open mouth.

Eric ran and the croc charged. The larger croc was now out of the water and giving chase. The smaller one lunged and bit down on Eric's calf. He screamed and collapsed on the ground. His calf felt like it was being crushed, the pressure sending waves of pain up his leg. The larger croc was nearly to him, moving in a purposely lazy stride.

The smaller croc began to pull with ferocious strength, trying to get his meal back into the water. Eric tried to hold himself steady by clawing at the sand but the croc was too strong and soon he was waist-deep in water. The croc began to twist his body and Eric was violently spun in the water, slamming his head into the riverbank as the croc tried to tear off his leg. He screamed as the larger croc moved in, its jaws open as it now lunged at his head.

The larger croc snarled and then retreated quickly into the water behind him.

The smaller croc let out a screech. Blood sprayed over Eric and the pressure on his leg went slack.

Eric saw only darkness at first. He thought the croc had bitten him in the face, but when he didn't feel pain, he recognized that the darkness was a shadow cast over him.

The creature was colossal, muscles rippling under gray fur. It stood as large as a horse but twice as thick and with large, powerful legs. The animal had its head in the organs of the smaller croc, which had been bitten in half. It was swallowing the croc's entrails. It picked up half the creature in its mouth and trotted a few feet away before dropping it on the ground and beginning to feed again.

Eric watched it eat. It lapped at the blood first, staining its face a dark red. It didn't seem to chew, just tear and swallow. Within seconds, half the croc was gone.

Eric moved as silently as he could. He pulled apart the limp jaws of the croc around his leg and slid up the soft dirt of the riverbank. Getting to his hands and knees, he crawled away from the creature and into the grass.

He froze. A growl had come from behind him. He slowly turned his head. The creature had finished half the croc and was eating the other half. The large croc was now on the other side of the river, silently watching the creature.

Eric got to his feet and ran. The grass whipped the bare skin on his torso and face and each step shot a surge of pain up his back. He ran until his legs burned and he was out of breath, pain in his side making him nearly double over. The bushes and tall grass were thick and he didn't feel like his arms had the strength to keep pushing them away from him. The skin on his arms and bare torso were cut and bleeding.

Something grabbed him, and he jumped and turned, hitting his foot on a rock in the process and collapsing onto his back. Will stood above him, surprise on his face as he leaned down to calm him.

"What is it?" Will said. "What's going on?"

Eric was out of breath and couldn't speak. He just pointed to the riverbank and Will glanced back toward it and stood up. He checked the chamber on his rifle.

"Stay put," he said.

Eric grabbed him. "Guns won't do anything."

36

Night came again and the darkness was always accompanied by a new wave of sounds. Insects and animals that slept during the day were now coming out into the fresh night air in search of food. Life itself seemed to grow louder on the Andhra Pradeshn plains when the sun went down.

Jalani sat next to a small fire she'd made from dried bark and twigs, sharpening her hunting knife with a smooth stone. Another fire was built a couple yards away, and Douglas lay in front of it, drunk as he was every night, with Sandra sitting next to him. They were laughing and telling stories and Sandra would put her hand on his shoulder when he said something particularly witty. Eventually, she began rubbing his arm as he told a long story of his time in New Zealand whale hunting.

Jalani thought of Eric and worry began to gnaw at her. It had not been her intention to like him or even get to know him. But he had an innocence about him that she found intriguing. It felt like she wanted to throw her arms around him and protect him from the world.

Dr. Namdi came and sat down next to Jalani, two cups

4

of tea in his hands. He handed one to her and stretched out his legs before the fire.

"You look sad," Jalani said.

"I could not save a boy tonight. His infection spread too fast. I just told his mother he was dead."

"Nothing is easy."

"No, nothing is." Namdi looked over to Sandra and Douglas. "You know, her husband is a quiet man but I think he will still kill the fat one when he returns."

Jalani chuckled. Then she grew sad and said, "If he returns."

"You do not think Thomas will kill this animal?" Namdi asked.

"I don't know."

"It is not like other animals I have seen."

"Yes, but Thomas is not like other hunters." She heard Sandra laugh and looked over to her before turning back to Namdi. "Let me ask you something; why are you still here? You could go to Paris or New York or London. Make lots of money and find a beautiful wife."

"I could," he said, "but that is not what I want. When I see these people suffer, I suffer with them. No one, even their own government, cares about them. They are seen as parasites because they live on the land and do not give taxes to the cities. But they are not parasites. They live *with* the land, not off of it. In harmony. They respect this place."

Jalani nodded and jabbed a stick in the fire, overturning a small log.

"Let me ask you something now," Namdi said. "You are a lovely girl. Why have you not married yet?"

"I don't know. I don't meet many eligible men in my work."

"Except Eric?"

Jalani looked at him, surprised at his perception.

"It is all right," Namdi said with a smile. "I will not tell Thomas if that is what worries you." He took a sip of tea. "He seems like a decent young man."

"He is. But he has much anger and confusion in him because of his father."

"Hm, I suppose we all do. Be careful in trying to heal him, Jalani. You may end up destroying the best part of him."

37

Will and Eric didn't stop to rest in the night. The sky was clear of clouds and the air was cool. To stop and wait for the heat of the morning would be foolish.

They made their way past the broad valley and climbed farther up into the lush highlands. The highlands were more a dense forest than anything else. The trees were thickly branched and the leaves ranged in colors from bright green to brown. Layers of cricket chirps and hoots from monkeys high up in the branches reverberated in the night.

"If I wasn't so damn scared," Will said, "I might really be in awe of how beautiful this is." He looked at Eric. He hadn't spoken since the incident at the river. "You okay?"

"Fine."

"You know, you haven't told me exactly what you saw."

"I wouldn't know how to describe it."

"Well, for starters, how big was it?"

"Maybe six or seven feet high, ten feet long."

"That's like twice the size of a bull."

"Trust me, it wasn't a bull."

The forest grew dense, and they had to push their way past thick foliage and bushes with long narrow thorns on every stem. Eric's legs itched from the dozens of small cuts and scrapes he'd accumulated.

"You know," Eric said, "when I was a kid I wasn't that great with girls. I was awkward and shy and they never paid attention to me or were usually just mean to me. My dad used to take me to baseball games. We didn't have a professional team, so we used to go to college games. There was this girl there that worked at the food stand. She was blonde and kinda skinny but had these gorgeous green eyes. I mean, I was only like twelve at the time but I thought I was full-on in love with her. I could never bring myself to talk to her, but she'd smile when she saw me and I'd smile back. I think she was the only girl at that time of my life that was nice to me.

"One of the games we went to she wasn't there. She wasn't at the next one either. She went to junior high school with one of my friends and I asked if he knew her and what happened. He said she moved. I still think about her sometimes, but I don't know why." He was silent a while. "I was really hoping one day to tell her how much those smiles meant to me."

They didn't speak again; the crunching of shrubbery under their feet filling the empty silence.

The sun seeped through the branches of the canopy above them at dawn. They'd walked the entire night without stopping. Now they were exhausted and hungry, with thirst making their stomachs twist in pain.

They stopped near a large boulder in a clearing and

sat down, their backs against the stone. A blanket of bird calls filled the forest and a colony of ants was busy at work on a tree stump in front of them.

Eric leaned back and closed his eyes. The heat felt wet in the forest and it soaked him. He hardly noticed when a glob of drool spattered on his chest. Another strand leaked down over his face and he opened his eyes.

Above him on the boulder was a face from his nightmares. The creature's eyes were drawn tight and its teeth were exposed. Eric couldn't move. He stared into the creature's eyes, watching its pupils dilate as its muscles tensed.

The creature lunged. Eric spun away on the ground, the horrible mouth snapping into empty air and missing his shoulder by a few inches. Will jumped and grabbed the rifle but the creature spun around too quickly and knocked him off his feet. It turned back to Eric and let out an earsplitting roar. Eric took off into the forest and the creature took after him.

The forest was thick. Eric couldn't see more than a few feet in front of him at a time. The branches scraped his face as he dashed through them, and the ground was uneven.

The creature pursued, adeptly moving through the density of the forest as if it were a bird. It ducked underneath low hanging branches and kept pace with its prey. Knocking small trees in its way over with thunderous crackling.

Eric tried to zigzag but ended up losing ground. He glanced back once at the creature; it was undoubtedly a hyena. It had the long forelegs and thick muscular build with the human-like eyes, but the size was unlike anything Eric had ever seen.

There was a tall tree with low branches in front of him and Eric leapt for the nearest branch, wrapping his arms around it and swinging his legs up. The beast flew into the air, its jaws wide, and snapped at Eric's legs but missed and bit into the branch, tearing half of it down with a loud crunch. Eric climbed to his knees and then up another branch, and then another. He looked down to see the creature eyeing him. It had intelligent eyes that sent a chill up Eric's back.

The beast crouched and then vaulted onto the tree, its claws catching the bark as it climbed to the first branch. Eric watched in horror as it rose to the next branch.

Eric climbed higher, the bark cutting his hands. When he neared the top, he looked down to see the beast's face staring back at him. The tree was leaning to the side under its weight, but still the creature climbed.

Eric got to the top and the animal was right behind him. He pulled out the handgun Jalani had given him and took aim. He fired once and missed but the second shot hit the animal above its right shoulder blade. The beast was caught off guard and fell on the branch underneath it.

A thunderous crunching echoed in the air as the tree nearly splintered in half. The creature crashed through the branches and onto the ground. The violent swaying of the tree made Eric lose his grip and he slammed into a branch on his way to the ground. He hit the dirt hard. He was next to the creature as it lay dazed. Eric stood and pain shot through his ankle, but he limped away as the hyena pushed itself up, a deep growl contorting its face with rage.

Eric came into a clearing and he darted for a precipice a couple dozen yards away. The beast was behind him, gaining on him with every second.

It was snarling wildly and drool sopped from its mouth. It almost had its prey now. The smell of its sweat was intoxicating and it opened its mouth, anticipating the warm flow of blood down its throat.

Eric flew off the ledge of the cliff and rolled down the steep side of the hill. The gun flew out of his hand in the tumble and slid down a dozen feet before coming to a stop. As he rolled, his body absorbed the impact of rocks and stray branches, but he saw the creature chasing after him, carefully managing its descent down the hill.

Eric crashed into the ground at the base of the hill, battered and in pain. He tried to rise, but his ankle gave out; it was likely broken. He collapsed onto his stomach as the massive hyena stood over him, its mouth lowering to clamp down on his ribcage.

A shot tore through the air and the beast yelped as a bullet from Will's rifle pierced its back leg. Another shot missed and hit the dirt ahead. The beast turned and let out a deep roar, anger and hatred filling its eyes. Another round struck its paw and it roared monstrously before sprinting into some nearby trees.

Will got down to Eric and bent over him. He put his arm around his waist and lifted.

A roar and trembling in the ground. The hyena raced out of a thicket of trees and leapt at Will. He held up his rifle and the beast bit down, crunching the wood and steel as if it were biting through a twig.

Another gunshot, this one more heavily bassed. Then another and another. Will flew off his feet and landed on his back, a gaping hole in his chest draining his body of blood. The hyena roared and lunged, but a series of shots filled the air. It collapsed on the ground not far from Eric with a heavy thud that seemed to shake the earth.

Thomas eased toward the beast, four tribesmen with rifles behind him. He held the barrel of the gun over the beast's heart and pulled the trigger, watching the blood flow into the dirt and stain it black. Eric saw Will vomiting blood. He stood up and limped over to him, sharp pain shooting through his ankle and legs.

"Will, come on. We're gonna get you help." He went to move him and Will let out a scream of pain. "Come on, Will," Eric said, tears filling his eyes, "come on, you're gonna be okay."

Will looked at him, a smile parting his bloodied lips. Life drained from his eyes, and his gurgled breathing stopped.

"No!" Eric shouted. He went to pick him up, but the weight was too much and he collapsed. "No! Will, come on. You're not gonna die, come on!"

"Let him go, boy," Thomas said.

Eric looked up to him, his eyes lit with rage. "You killed him."

"We were trying to shoot the beast."

"You told me you don't miss. You killed him."

"Don't be ridiculous." He knelt down and picked Eric up by the arm, placing it over his neck to bear his weight. "People die here, Eric." Thomas told the tribesmen to bury Will and then said, "Come on, we'll get you to a doctor."

38

Jalani had driven Douglas and Sandra to the village after one of the tribesmen fetched them. They came upon a village in celebration, the men that had hunted with Thomas being hailed as warriors.

Fires were lit, and mountains of flesh were being cooked as a feast was anticipated. The hide of the beast hung on a vine tied between two trees and was as large as a tent. Its head was mounted on a post and children were throwing stones at it. The primitive music of the tribe— little more than plucked strings on handmade sitars and leather-bound tablas—was wailing in the late afternoon sun.

Eric sat with a primitive brace made of wood and rope around his ankle. The pain was soothed with a type of leaf they'd given him to chew. It was dizzying and obviously a narcotic, but it felt pleasant and made him feel warm and calm. He watched Thomas tell Sandra about Will and her cold, distant reaction. Douglas sat next to a fire and pulled out a bottle of liquor and passed it around to the hunters who had killed the great beast.

Jalani sat next to Eric. "They now consider you a man," she said.

He didn't feel like a man. He didn't feel like much of anything. Just a cold, gray weight in his belly and dizziness in his head. Will was a good man; he didn't deserve to die like that. Eric understood it was a mistake but he didn't deserve that. He'd saved Eric's life and now he was gone.

"I didn't kill it."

"No, but you showed courage in the hunt. That's what's important. To have courage in the face of death. That's what a warrior is." Jalani waited for a response, but Eric gave none so she leaned down and gently kissed his cheek. "I am glad you're safe."

The feast got underway and the meat was skewered on smooth sticks and passed around. There was a boiling pot in which the beast's heart was carefully cut as a priest chanted a prayer. Pieces of the heart were given to all the hunters, a portion going to Thomas. He ate the meat with his eyes closed, blood dripping down his chin like one of his savage ancestors. Afterward, he came to where Eric was seated.

"He was a good man, but bad things often happen out here," Thomas said, sitting down next to him.

"You killed him on purpose."

"I swear to you, I did not mean to kill that man. He was my friend, Eric. And what possible reason would I have for doing so? He was a paying customer, a good paying customer. The truth is, the tribesmen are not as well trained on rifles as we are. It's a new technology for them and they take it too lightly. But I take full responsibility. I should not have told them to fire when you two were in harm's way. I'm sorry I caused you this pain."

Eric looked over to a group of children eating the meat on thin sticks. "Sandra doesn't seem very pissed off at you."

"She will grieve in her own way." Thomas rose, taking something out of his pocket and handing it to Eric. "I wanted you to have this."

It was one of the creature's teeth fastened on a piece of leather to make a necklace. "Thanks."

Thomas nodded and walked away. Some of the children ran up to him and yelled requests. He lamented and picked up a stone. Taking aim at about twenty yards away, he threw the stone and hit the creature's head on the post. The children erupted in awe and laughter.

You never miss, Eric thought.

39

The celebration lasted well into the night. The meat that wasn't eaten was hung over the thick vine and smoked dry. The hide was cut up. Jalani told Eric it would be used as clothing and the bones would be made into jewelry. Nothing was wasted.

Eric woke in the middle of the night. An image kept coming to him: Will lying on the ground, his blood soaking the earth. It didn't let him sleep. The whole incident replayed in his head over and over. The smell of gunpowder and blood, the bassed sound of large rifles, Will's last breaths.

Eric stood using a wooden crutch the villagers had carved out of a branch for him. He hobbled outside the tent and stood in the night. The moon was high and lit the valley before him in pale light. There were herds of gazelle and deer grazing in the tall grass. He looked around the village; it was empty and the fires were all out except for one at the end. He hoped Jalani was still awake.

Eric slowly limped over, the bare wood of the crutch

digging into the flesh of his underarm. A breeze was blowing and it felt cool against the burnt skin on his face. Snoring was coming from some of the tents he passed, a few groans of pleasure coming from others. He made his way to the last fire and looked into the tent.

Sandra's nude body lay on a bed of fur. Thomas was on top of her, kissing her passionately, his hands caressing her body. Eric stood frozen a moment as he realized what he was seeing and then moved away from the tent.

An epiphany screamed in his head and he had to sit down on a nearby stone to quiet it down. He looked toward the tent, disgust and guilt going through him in waves. He finally stood up and limped back to his tent.

The next morning came quietly, most of the village sleeping off their drunkenness well into midday. Douglas told Eric they would be leaving soon. Another jeep had been brought from Kavali and they would be going back there.

Eric hadn't slept for more than a few hours. His dreams were filled with blood and laughter and screams. He saw Will's torn body. It was standing upright and speaking to him, trying to say something but no sound was coming out. The flesh was so severely torn on his face that Eric didn't recognize him at first. He said something and then collapsed.

Eric rose and shuffled out of the tent. His ankle felt better though the swelling hadn't gone down. His calf burned from where the croc had bitten down.

The sun was already cooking the plains and the cool breeze of last night had been replaced with a wall of boiling heat. He looked out over the valley before him, observing the contrast between the sapphire blue sky and the green grass below. A leopard stood over a gazelle, carefully glancing around every few seconds to make sure nothing was trying to spirit away her kill. She looked up once and saw Eric on top of the plateau.

"Come on, Eric," Douglas said, "we're riding with Thomas."

They loaded everything in their jeep and Eric sat in the back. Jalani had left with Sandra and Namdi an hour before and her jeep was already well out of sight.

Thomas checked a few tents, presumably to say goodbye, and then hopped into the driver's seat and started the engine. Douglas sat in the passenger seat. They pulled away from the village and slowly made their way down the side of the plateau, Thomas carefully applying the brakes to keep from gaining too much speed. Occasionally they would slide, and he would turn the wheel sharply left or right, causing the jeep to twist to its side and come to a halt. But they made their way down and the jeep chugged along the dirt path.

Eric pulled out the handgun Jalani had given him. He aimed it at the back of Thomas's head.

His hand began to shake and a familiar choking sensation came over him. It was hard to breathe. He felt the weight of the gun in his palm. Thomas's gray hair ended above his neck and sweat rolled down his head and soaked his collar.

Eric lowered the gun and tossed it onto the seat next to him.

40

They rode in silence for a couple of hours. They had to stop and wait for a herd of kiang, a type of Asian donkey, to cross their path. The large females circled the younger ones to protect them from the strange mechanical beast in their midst. Douglas climbed out and urinated on a bush.

"Did she come to you to kill him or did you go to her?" Eric said, looking off in the distance at a glimmering river.

"Pardon?"

"When you killed Will, was it more for you or her?"

"Stop talking nonsense, boy. I'm sorry, he was a good man. But I had—"

"I saw you together in the tent last night."

Thomas looked back at him in the rearview and then looked forward again. "They had a loveless marriage. She's wasn't that heartbroken and she didn't need to be."

Douglas came back and they started off. A red Volkswagen bus crossed their path and Thomas stopped and chatted a while. They were Canadian tourists looking to film a pride of Asiatic lions and he recommended the Gir Forest, almost a hundred kilometers from where they stood.

Another hour into the drive and Douglas was already drunk, telling longwinded stories about his adventures. Eric surmised that he had him figured out. He didn't actually care about adventure, he cared about telling others about his adventures. He lived through what others saw of him. He lived only in their eyes. At that moment, Douglas made him sick.

The grass became taller—at least chest high—and the path turned into a decent dirt road but became narrower.

There was an object ahead in the road but it was too far off to make out exactly what it was. It looked like a large animal, but it wasn't moving. As they approached, Eric made out the sharp contours of the other jeep. It was flipped upside down.

Thomas stopped the jeep. There were bloodstains across the wheels and on the dirt around the vehicle. The engine was smoking and supplies were scattered across the road.

Eric felt sick.

Jalani.

Eric jumped out of the jeep and ran over, getting on his hands and knees and looking into the wreckage. Douglas and Thomas were out and tried to help.

"Eric, help us flip the jeep."

They stood on one side and pushed. The metal groaned as the vehicle tipped. Eric felt his muscles strain as he dug in with his feet into the soft dirt and put his shoulder against the jeep. The vehicle reached the tipping point and flipped back, its tires crashing into the dirt. Nothing was underneath.

"Sandra!" Thomas yelled out over the grass. "Sandra!"

Douglas started blaring the horn of the jeep. He

2

stopped a few seconds to listen and then started again. Thomas took out his rifle from their jeep along with a pistol from a leather satchel.

"Where are you going?" Douglas said.

"To find them."

"In what direction? They could be anywhere. Best to wait here."

Thomas hung the rifle strap over his shoulder. "Take the boy and look up the road a few kilometers. Then come back here and wait for me."

Eric rode with Douglas up the road. Douglas would honk the horn every five or ten seconds and then wait for a response. They managed to attract the attention of a herd of gazelles that stood under the shade of a tree watching them, but nothing else.

"They probably had an accident," Douglas said, more to himself than Eric. "Jalani must've been drunk."

They drove for five kilometers and spotted nothing. Just animals, grass, trees and the blue open sky. Douglas turned around and headed back.

"What's the matter?" Douglas said. "You used to be quite talkative... I'm sure they're fine, we'll find them. I suppose you're still upset about Will's death too, eh? It was an honest mistake, Eric. It could've happened to anyone."

"Suppose so," Eric said flatly.

They came back to the sight of the overturned jeep and Douglas shut off the engine. Birds were high up in the nearby trees singing, but other than that the plains were silent. There was no breeze and the heat sat on them and cooked.

176

"You know, that creature," Douglas said. "I think I know what it was."

"It wasn't a hyena?"

"No, it was. But it was obviously far too large to be the spotted hyena it appeared. I'd read about something once called Hyaenodon. It's the ancestor of the hyena, only much larger. I wonder if it could still exist out here?"

"The villagers think it's punishment from God."

"Yes," Douglas pulled out a flask and took a drink, "that it might be."

Douglas pressed the horn and stopped a few seconds later. Noon turned into afternoon and afternoon into the evening as they sat in the jeep, drinking water and eating snack chips and dried meat, soaking their shirts in water and wrapping it around their heads to keep the sun off.

When the sun went down and darkness descended, sparkling stars covering the tar-black sky. The air cooled, but not by as much as Eric had hoped and sweat still poured out of him. He went to take a drink out of his bottle of water and it was empty. He tossed it onto the floor of the jeep.

"How long do you think we should wait?" Douglas said, obviously losing his nerve. "I don't like sitting out here in the dark."

"You want to leave?" Eric said, amused. "I thought Thomas was your friend?"

"He is, of course," Douglas said. "I'm just saying there's not much we can do just sitting out here like bait."

Their heads turned simultaneously. Out past a small thicket of trees came a sound that had burned itself into Eric's mind: maniacal laughter.

41

Darkness covered the plains, but Thomas pressed forward. He searched the tall grass with his rifle held in front of him. One of the big cats roared in the distance, a leopard probably. Sometimes he'd hear the hollering of macaques, but they were rare.

"Sandra!" he yelled out, against his better judgment. He wasn't exactly confident that he expected a response.

Thomas stopped underneath a tree and sat down, exhaustion weakening his legs and making his feet ache. The moon was bright and full. It reminded him of his drunken days in Africa, watching the full moon through the jungle canopy, unsure what day it was and not really caring.

He rose and continued his search.

There was little in the night that could surprise him any longer. He knew the calls of every animal out there. But he was taken aback by the creature he'd killed yesterday. He'd heard rumors from the tribesmen for years about giant hyenas that stole children in the night, but how could one believe in such stories?

He was more frightened than he let on. What else was

out there?

As he made his way through the grass, he became acutely aware that something else was with him. Whenever he'd move forward, he'd hear the grass behind him parting.

He took a few steps forward and heard the sound again. Thomas took a deep breath, and quickly dropped to one knee, spinning around with the rifle held in front of him. But the grass was empty; the wind rustling through a few of the taller strands.

He lowered his rifle and stood up. Glancing around, he could see that he hadn't been following any sort of trail for quite some time. He was wandering aimlessly, breaking the first rule of searching the plains: Always have an exit plan.

Walking back through the grass, he saw movement in the periphery of his vision; a roving mass just to the left, a few meters away. He could tell by the width of the part in the grass that it was massive.

Thomas raised his rifle and took aim. The mass was moving closer, creeping slowly through the tall grass, hardly making a sound.

It was stalking him.

His finger lightly pressed on the trigger, not pulling it the entire way until he had a clear shot and knew what he was hitting. The movement in the grass slowed and then stopped. It was gone.

Thomas kept his eyes fixed on where he had last seen the movement. It must've spotted him. He steadied the rifle and fired. A whine sounded as a leopard leapt into the air, its body twisting as it startled. The lithe body of the cat landed in the grass and it hurried away.

Thomas breathed a sigh of relief and went toward

where the leopard had been. They were ferocious creatures; he'd seen one take down a wildebeest in Kenya by itself. There were even stories of them killing adult gorillas. Injured, they were downright unpredictable. He saw the leopard hobbling to a nearby tree and he raised his rifle and took a step forward.

As he did, he felt something soft giving way underfoot. Glancing down, he saw a cylindrical shape underneath his boot. He bent down and picked it up, bringing it into the moonlight. It felt rubbery and wet.

It was a severed arm. Torn from its socket.

Thomas dropped the arm, a quiet gasp escaping him. It was the arm of a Caucasian female, the nails painted red. The flesh looked gray and fell off the bone.

He looked at it a moment longer and then turned away, choking back his emotion. Slinging the rifle over his shoulder, he started making his way back to the jeep.

42

Eric sat still in the jeep, his heart beating quickly and pounding in his ears. The laughter they'd heard had stopped, and silence replaced it. Not even the crickets made noise. It was a terrible silence, unnatural. It sent shivers up his back.

"Maybe we should drive off for a while," Douglas said. "Then we'll circle back and try to find Thomas."

Eric nodded, not taking his eyes off the tall grass and forest in the distance. Douglas started the engine and instantly there was a roar and cacophony of laughter. A massive hyena sprang out of the trees.

Eric flew over Douglas as the beast rammed its head into the jeep, causing two of its tires to lift off the ground. He rammed it again and the metal bent as the jeep flipped over onto its side.

Douglas screamed as his leg was crushed under the weight of the vehicle. Eric was thrown out and hit the dirt. The beast circled around the vehicle, drool pouring out of its mouth in long strands as it spotted Douglas on the ground.

It approached, a low growl escaping before it twisted into a laugh.

Douglas' screams pierced the night air as the animal put its mouth over his head and bit down. The loud crunch of his skull and the spatter of blood over the animal's head caused bile to rise in Eric's throat and he stood and ran.

He hobbled along the dirt road, his ankle throbbing with pain, and could see shapes in the grass chasing him. They would run ahead of him and then stop and let him pass just to run ahead again. The laughter was at a fever pitch, saturating the air. It was coming from both sides of the road.

Another hyena dove out of some trees in front of him and Eric nearly ran into it. He avoided the beast's mouth and ran behind him into the grass. The animal turned and was after him.

Eric let the grass whip his body as he dashed through it, not looking back. The laughter was circling him, running ahead of him and closing in from behind. He turned sharply to the right and then up, trying to zigzag. To place where the animals were by their laughter. But they followed his movements and ran ahead of him again.

He could see light up ahead and gradually saw the shape of a house outside the patch of grass he was in. Calling on the last of his strength, he dug deep and sprinted.

Eric burst out of the grass and onto a flat clearing. Ten yards away was a white house with a large porch. He darted for it, hearing the snarls of the animals behind him. The porch light was on and it seemed like a beacon in the darkness. His legs were failing him and he was slowing down but he felt the wood of the steps as he ran up the porch and to the front door. It was locked.

A living room window was near the door. Eric covered his face and jumped through. The glass shattered and scraped his body and he felt the sting of cuts from his face down to his shins. He stood and ran as he heard a roar in the darkness behind him.

The house was cluttered and messy. Bloodstains covered the floors and walls. Eric ran past a small kitchen and saw a closet door in the hallway. He opened it and jumped inside, shutting the door behind him.

The closet was small and smelled like linen and dust. With his back against some shelves, it gave him only enough room so that his body wasn't pressed against the wood of the door.

His breathing was too loud and he tried to quiet it. He put his ear to the door and listened. It was silent at first and then he heard the deafening crash of the door smashed to bits. Then glass from the broken window crunching under the weight of something. Slowly, the sound of deep pants approached him. He could hear the beast sniffing, trying to pick up a scent.

Eric looked down to the crack between the floor and the closet door; some light was coming through and he saw a shadow coming close. The panting grew loud as the animal stood in front of the door. It stopped and took in a deep breath through its nostrils. The snout leaned down and sniffed at the floor. Eric held his breath.

Suddenly, the sniffing stopped and the beast moved on and was gone. Eric exhaled and every muscle inside him relaxed. As he took a deep breath, the ear-piercing sound of splintering wood tore through the night and the beast's head rammed through the closet door, missing Eric's stomach by a few inches.

Eric was pinned against the shelves. He shoved his thumb into the animal's eye, causing it to howl in pain. The hyena thrashed violently and withdrew its head far enough for Eric to open the door and slip out. There was a staircase in the hallway and he ran up as the hyena's roar echoed through the house. He got to the top of the stairwell and looked back; the beast was at the bottom of the stairs staring up at him.

He dashed through the hallway and felt something grip his shoulder.

"Eric!"

Jalani grabbed him and pulled him into a room. They ran to the back and Jalani led him up a ladder that went to the attic. They climbed and Jalani pulled the ladder up when they were in the attic, shutting off the entrance with a small wooden door and latch.

The beast crashed through the bedroom door and tore apart the room, howling in frustration and bloodlust at its escaped prey. It ripped the bed apart and smashed the closets before stopping and staring up at the hatch leading to the attic.

Eric stumbled and then wrapped his arms around her. She smelled of dirt and grass and blood.

"I thought you were dead," he said out of breath.

"I lived," Jalani said. "But maybe not for long."

43

Thomas walked along the dirt road, listening to the crickets. He saw a dark shape up ahead. It was the jeep. And behind it was the other one.

He froze in his tracks and looked around as he brought his rifle up. He cautiously made his way to the jeeps. He could see the remains of Douglas' corpse, little more than legs caught under the jeep and some blood-stained rags that had been his clothes.

He knelt and picked up the torn shirt, observing the significant bite marks across the chest before dropping it. Thomas sighed and stood up. Off in the distance he heard laughter. It was over a large patch of grass. He took Douglas' rifle and slung it across his chest before walking toward the sounds.

The grass hid him well if he crouched low. He kept his breathing to a whisper and stopped every few paces to make sure nothing was following him. When he reached the edge of the grass before a tree line, he could see a house with the porch light on. In front of it were three colossal hyenas.

They were snapping at each other and rolling around in the dirt. One bit the other's leg and it let out a whelp before nipping at the other's ear.

The beasts rolled and nipped and eventually grew bored. They sat on the ground surveying their surroundings and staring up at the small window of the attic. One finally rose and walked inside the house. The other two promptly lay on their sides and fell asleep.

Thomas stepped backward into the grass, keeping his eye on the two hyenas sprawled out on the ground. They were obviously juveniles. The one they'd killed the other night was large and male. That meant a matriarch was still out there. If these were like normal spotted hyenas, the matriarch would be the largest and most aggressive of the clan.

Another step and a crunch. He looked down and saw he'd stepped on a piece of dry bark. One of the hyenas looked up, straining its neck and moving its ears to pick up any more sound. Thomas stood entirely still, not even breathing. He could feel sweat rolling down his back, tickling his skin.

The hyena lay its head back down, ignoring the sound. Thomas breathed and slowly turned, moving as quickly as he could in a crouch.

A growl tore through the silence of the night. Thomas stopped, hearing the deep breathing of the creature right behind him. He turned his head and saw the two juveniles on the edge of the grass, glaring at him with their red eyes, snarling.

Thomas raised his gun in a slow, purposeful motion, aiming at the juvenile closest to him. The hyenas took a step forward and then hesitated. They let out mournful whines and ducked their heads low. Then they backed away from the grass and sat down on the ground.

Thomas's brow furrowed and he lowered the rifle.

The hyenas were still. They kept their eyes low, as if frightened.

He felt the breath first.

It was hot and wet against the skin on his neck. Drool slid down his back and he heard rumbling coming from an enormous belly. He didn't turn around; he just closed his eyes and felt the wetness of a mouth closing around him.

44

Eric sat with his back against a wall of the attic, Jalani asleep in his arms. She had smears of dirt on her face and clothes, but her beauty still shone through like an emerald gleaming through water. He had no watch but could guess that it was probably three or four in the morning. He'd been hearing howls and laughter all night. The hyenas weren't leaving; they would circle the house, sometimes coming inside and occasionally into the room below.

Eric stayed up until sunrise. The light came through the window and filled the attic. Swirls of dust were in every beam and the room had the smell of mildew.

The attic was small and dirty, cluttered with old papers and clothes from vacationers not terribly worried about leaving behind personal items. There was some lingerie in a corner coated with a thick layer of dust, and cardboard boxes filled with old paperback novels, brushes, matchbooks, toiletries, and a few office supplies. In the north corner were a stool and a three-gallon plastic container of gasoline with a funnel.

Jalani awoke and smiled when she saw him. She

rubbed her eyes and yawned, a grave expression coming over her face when the realities of her circumstances dawned on her, and she realized it wasn't a dream.

"Did you not sleep?" she asked.

"I'm fine."

"You can sleep now if you like."

"No, I'm okay." He glanced around the attic. "We should empty those boxes and see if we can find anything useful."

They went about the task of dumping the contents of all the boxes onto the bare floor. Soon, hardly any portion of the floor was visible. A hunting knife was in one box. Eric tucked it into his waistband. They found an old pack of gum and each had a piece, the gum stale and tasting like dust.

Eventually, everything was emptied on the floor and examined. There was little they could use.

"We'll need to leave here soon," Eric said, going to the window and glaring out.

"They won't leave."

He turned to her. "How do you know?"

"We've killed one of their clan. They won't leave until we're dead."

Eric turned back to the window. He noticed something out near the grass: a white shirt and boots. They were Thomas' boots.

"Stay here," Eric said, running to the hatch. He opened the latch and went to climb down.

Jalani grabbed him and shouted, "No!" She pulled him up just as massive jaws snapped shut below his feet. It jumped again, the snout coming up through the hatch. It knocked Eric up and over Jalani.

They crawled to the other side of the room and listened as the hyena thumped its snout against the ceiling, growling and biting at the hatch but unable to get its teeth into it.

Jalani wrapped her arms around him and they sat in silence, listening to the growls fade and the beating of the creature's footsteps as it exited the room and left the house.

"Those things are the devil," Jalani whispered.

Eric, unable to catch his breath, put his hand on her arm and closed his eyes, his heart feeling like it was about to burst out of his chest.

45

They sat in the corner of the attic most of the day.

Soon, their bellies ached with hunger and their lips were cracking from lack of water. Out here, even indoors, dehydration could occur after hours, not days. Eric looked out the window. One of the hyenas was asleep on the ground. It lay on its side, its belly moving up and down in shallow breaths. He didn't see the others.

"We need to get out of here," Eric said.

"How?"

"This window. We can climb out onto the roof and maybe sneak away."

"They would hear us."

"It's better than staying here and starving to death."

Eric grabbed a folding chair that was leaned against the wall and slammed it against the window, shattering the glass.

"Stay here," Eric said.

He climbed out of the small window, cutting his hands on the shards of glass that had scattered on the pane. The roof was tiled with shingles and clean, no debris and little dirt. He moved slowly, going up to the middle of the roof which ended at a point, before surveying the land around him.

The jeeps were off about a hundred yards, through a thick patch of grass. On the one he had driven in, only the exterior had been damaged. If they could get to it and tip it over it should still be in running condition.

One of the hyenas stepped out of the house and looked up to the roof. It roared at the sight of Eric and he stumbled backward and nearly fell. He made his way to the window and climbed in as the hyena began to pace back and forth in front of the house.

"I found a way," Eric said as he climbed in. "If we can make it to the jeeps one should still be running."

"How are we going to do that?"

"I don't know yet," Eric said.

He stared at the animals in the front yard. There were two of them there now. The heat was getting to them as well. They were panting heavily and their mouths were dry. One of them went and laid in the shade of a tree, glancing up occasionally at the house and then putting his head back on the ground.

The other sat in front of the house and stared at the window.

Eric scavenged through the items in the attic once more and didn't find much that was useful. Jalani lay on her side and watched him. Eric was reminded again of just how exotically beautiful she was. It was amazing to him that she was a hunter for a living. When he thought of a hunter, he thought of Thomas or the tough-as-leather fishermen off the coast of Mexico. Not a thin young woman that could've just as easily been on a runway as in the plains of India.

"Maybe there's food in the basement?" she said.

Eric froze. "These houses have basements?"

"Yes."

He glanced around; everything was made of wood. "Are the stairs leading down to the basement made of wood?"

"I don't know."

Eric ran to the window and looked down. The sun was still high and they had hours of light left. The hyenas were both under the shade of the tree, watching a flock of birds in the sky.

"You have to climb out there and draw their attention," he said.

"What?"

"Just yell and throw stuff at 'em."

"Why?"

"I'm going to the basement."

"Are you crazy?"

"I'm not letting us die in this dirty little room, Jalani." He put his arm around her and pressed his lips to hers. "Please," he said.

Jalani climbed out of the window. Eric handed her armfuls of things to throw. He leaned out the window and kissed her again and as he turned away she grabbed him.

"Be careful," she said.

"I will. Just keep them off me a few minutes."

Jalani began yelling and the hyenas growled and approached. They stood watching, mouths agape with yellow, jagged teeth. Jalani took a brush and threw it, missing. One hyena walked to the brush and sniffed it, turning back to Jalani.

She took a paperback novel and hit him in the head.

The animal let out a ferocious roar that drew another hyena out of the house.

Eric watched from the window, and as soon as all three were in front of the house, he ran back and grabbed the container of gas and some matches that were in a box. He opened the hatch leading to the bedroom and climbed down.

Claw marks had scraped most of the glossy finish off the floors, and the bed was destroyed, lying in pieces around the room and in the hallway. The walls were torn apart.

He walked carefully, each creak in the floor sending a shot of adrenaline through him. The sounds of the animals outside echoed through the house. He made his way into the hall and past a bathroom.

The first-floor kitchen had beige floor tiling and white walls. There was a calendar up on the fridge and it had some writing on it. On the far side of the room was a door. He walked to it, ducking below a window over the sink, and opened it. Wooden stairs led down to a basement.

Eric softly closed the door behind him. It was dark, but there was some light coming through a ground-level window. He opened the plastic container of gasoline and poured it over the steps, one at a time, as he made his way down. He coated every step until it was dripping with gas and poured the last of it on the beams that supported the stairs.

The basement was just as cluttered as the attic but had larger items. There was an old lawnmower, tools, metal shelves filled with electrical replacement parts and a rifle hanging up over a workbench. He ran to it and checked the chamber. It was empty and he searched the shelves until he found a box of ammunition. The rifle was just a .22 caliber, hardly enough to pierce the flesh of those things, but enough to get their attention.

Eric ran up the steps and into the kitchen. He looked out the window over the sink and saw the hyenas worked up to a frenzy, the debris Jalani had thrown dotting the ground around them. He smashed the butt of his rifle through the glass and the animals stopped their display and turned toward the sound. Eric took aim and fired a shot into the chest of the largest one, causing him to roar with anger. The other two sprinted for the house and Eric ran in front of the basement door.

The two beasts smashed their way through the living room and stood in the hallway, watching Eric. The hyena he'd shot came in and spotted him, its mouth opening and revealing knife-sized fangs. It darted for him.

Eric got off two shots, one missing and one hitting its mark in the eye. The hyena roared and fell into a wall, causing a large hole as the other two hopped over him.

Eric ran into the basement and shut the door. He jumped down the stairs and sprinted to the back of the large space, behind a metal shelf packed with tools. The door burst open; raining splinters on the floor below. The three hyenas leapt down the stairs. Their anger had caused them to go into a fury, and they would bite at each other and bare their teeth. They stood sniffing the air and then began searching the basement.

Two rummaged through a stack of cardboard boxes, but the large one stood in the center of the basement, looking from one item to the next. It held its head up, the muscles in its neck straining, and inhaled deeply through its nostrils. It went to the side of the basement Eric was on.

195

The hyena carefully scanned the space in front of it. It searched from top to bottom and took a few paces back. A chill went up Eric's back as its eyes scanned over where he was and kept going. The hyena smelled the air again and turned away.

Suddenly, it spun and dashed for the shelf. Its head thrust in between two shelves and into Eric's ribs, scraping his flesh as its teeth clamped down and tore through his shirt. The other two hyenas pounced and tore at the shelf, trying to bite through the metal.

Eric saw that the shelf was attached to the wall by two metal bars bolted to each side. He kicked at one and it bent. He kicked again and it broke away, the bolt clinking as it hit the gray cement of the basement floor. He broke the other one and pushed.

The hyenas had almost forced their way through now, one of their heads snapping at Eric's arms. Eric put his legs up against the shelf and thrust out. The shelf tipped and fell on the animals with a thunderous crash.

Eric ran for the stairs as the hyenas shook off the pain and started for him. The large one leapt at him with its jaws wide, and he ducked, causing it to hit the wall snout first and land hard on the floor.

Eric climbed the steps and took out a matchbook. He struck one and threw it on the stairs, and they burst into flame. The fire was spreading quickly. Eric had to bolt for the kitchen as the heat wafted up and singed his face.

The hyena leapt at him just as the flames caught its face, searing its sensitive eyes and snout. The beast howled and fell backward, blinded by the fire. The other two ran over, staying clear of the flames. One looked up and saw Eric running out the door. It leapt at him in an act of rage and desperation, crashing into the center of the stairs. It'd soaked up the gasoline in its fur and the fire spread over its soft belly and eventually its face, causing it to fall from the stairs and dart around the room, crashing into everything in its path as it panicked from the agony.

Eric slammed the door behind him and stood against it, out of breath, his legs starting to sting from the flames. He looked down at his left arm and saw a large gash and blood. Taking off his shirt, he wrapped it around the wound tightly and headed to the bedroom upstairs.

46

Eric and Jalani sat at the dining room table and gorged themselves on what food they could find and water from the kitchen faucet. The groceries in the fridge had rotted, but the cupboards had plenty of dry cereal and crackers.

They could hear the hyenas howling in the basement below, the occasional thud as one of their bodies fell back to the cement floor from a failed jump. The stairs had burnt and crumbled, but the fire hadn't moved up to the rest of the house yet; though it had filled the house with smoke. Soon, they would have to leave.

The hyenas were trapped. Jalani told him that in the days ahead after the strongest killed and ate the other two, the last would die of starvation. If the smoke didn't kill them first.

She reached across the table and caressed his hand. He took her hand in his.

"Thomas had money," she said. "A lot of money. Most of it in accounts in Hyderabad. I think I can get it out."

Eric nodded, looking out the window. "I'll be right back," he said. He'd forgotten entirely about Thomas.

"Where you going?"

"It'll just take a second."

He walked outside and to Thomas' clothing. They were torn and stained with dark blood. Eric found a soft patch of earth and got on his knees. He dug a hole with his hands, deep enough to fit the shirt and boots. He placed them inside and covered the hole. He stood up and wiped at the dirt on himself, looking down at the makeshift grave.

Eric stood for some time, watching the grass sway in a light breeze around the home, and then went back inside. Jalani was lying on the couch, half-asleep. Her body would jolt whenever one of the hyenas roared and she would wake.

Eric gently caressed her cheek and said, "We need to go."

They took the rifle and all the food they could find, dumped out a rotten gallon of milk and filled the container with water, and headed out to the jeeps.

The breeze was cool and flocks of birds chirped their songs in the trees. A jet flew high overhead, leaving a white streak across the sky. The plains were alive with sound and motion. White clouds were scattered across the blue sky with the sun bright at its apex.

There wasn't much left in the jeeps. All the food had been taken by whatever animals had crossed here, and the water jugs were either torn apart or gone. Eric went to the jeep where Douglas' corpse had been. Animals had left little of that too.

With Eric on the end and Jalani pushing on the hood, the metal of the jeep groaned as it was forced back to a horizontal position, landing hard on its tires and kicking up clouds of dirt. Eric examined the tires, and they all

Shigeru Brody

looked okay. The keys were in the ignition and the jeep started on the second try. Jalani climbed into the passenger seat and leaned back.

The matriarch hyena vaulted out of the grass and landed next to the jeep, her colossal weight making the vehicle tremble. Jalani screamed and twisted her body away as the creature snapped at her and its teeth dug into the seat, tearing out a chunk as it pulled away.

The massive jaws lunged and bit into the metal frame of the jeep which grated as her teeth bent the metal and tore a piece away.

Eric grabbed the rifle and shoved the barrel into the creature's mouth as it came in for another bite. The hyena bit down on the barrel as he pulled the trigger inside its mouth and the beast stumbled backward, the gun still in its teeth.

The tires dug into the earth as Eric floored the accelerator. The hyena bit through the rifle, shattering it into pieces before starting after them.

Clouds of dirt were kicking up behind the jeep, making it difficult to see, but the outline of the gigantic creature was still visible. It was larger than anything Eric could've imagined: the size of an elephant, with thick musculature and fangs the size of steak knives that protruded out of an enormous mouth.

Eric glanced down and saw he only had half a tank of gas. There were no more jugs of fuel left. Thomas had told him about hyenas. They couldn't run fast, but they could run far. The gas would eventually run out and it might catch up.

He pressed down on the accelerator as far as it would go, the jeep thrashing about on the uneven road. It got far enough away from the beast that he had some time.

"When I stop the jeep you need to run."

"No," Jalani said.

"I need to do this."

"Eric—"

"Trust me on this. I can do it. Just run when I say."

He waited another minute, and then slammed on the brakes. "Run!"

Jalani hesitated and then jumped out. She ran to the jungle and waited for him.

"Go! Don't wait for me."

Eric climbed out of the jeep and took off his shirt from around the wound on his arm and tore it into thin pieces. He went to the back of the jeep and unscrewed the gas cap. He rolled up some of the pieces and pushed them down as far as they would go into the gas tank. Pulling them back out, he saw it had a little bit of gasoline on the tip.

The hyena was almost on him, only a few dozen feet away. It didn't stop to consider its prey; it just charged. Fury was in its eyes as it barreled toward Eric, drool sopping from it gargantuan mouth.

Eric took out the matches and lit the cloth. The flame began to work its way down the fabric. He shoved the pieces of cloth as far into the gas tank as it would go. He climbed up onto the hood and took out the knife he'd found in the attic.

The beast was enormous. It stood nearly as tall as a basketball rim and was thickly muscled, its jaws bulging underneath thin gray fur. It galloped like a horse, but because of its size, its gait was awkward. An uneven back and forth between its fore and hind legs.

Eric crouched low on the hood, sweat stinging his eyes.

The great beast leapt into the air and slammed into the jeep, knocking Eric onto his back and flattening two tires of the vehicle. It pressed its face down on Eric and he shoved the knife into its mouth vertically, keeping it from being able to close. The animal pulled away, the knife jabbing into its tongue and upper jaw, and bit down. The blade bent and the handle shattered.

Eric looked at the cloth; it was burned down past where he could see. The hyena lunged for him and he rolled off the jeep and onto the ground. He managed to get to his feet as the hyena bent low to spring.

The explosion threw Eric forward and his back screamed as the skin was charred. The animal howled in pain, its soft skin lit aflame. It fell off the jeep and roared, blinded from the blast, its eyes liquefied. It snapped wildly at the air, trying to bite down on anything it could, and then darted in one direction, smashing into a tree and knocking it to the ground. It went in another direction, dazed, and collapsed with a roar.

Eric crawled away and lay on the dirt, the pain in his back and legs nearly making him pass out. He watched as the creature's immense body burned in the dirt, black smoke rising into the air and whirling into the breeze. The beast was spasming and violently thrashing from side-to-side. It slowed as the fire burned and it inhaled the smoke, charring its throat and lungs. It moved one last time, a paw gently scratching in the ground, its savagery having been eaten away in the fire.

Its breathing stopped as the flames suffocated it, and consumed what was left.

After a few minutes, he heard a rustle behind him and turned to see Jalani.

As she helped him up, he felt the softness of her skin

and could feel her heart beating against him. The sun had painted the sky a glowing crimson in its retreat, and a tiger was roaring somewhere. Beauty and death, like Will had said. But Eric realized that Will had been mistaken about something. He'd never realized that the difference wasn't in the plains; it was in us.

The plains were indifferent to them both.

47

Eric sat on the 747 jumbo jet and popped two pain-killers as he leaned his head back and closed his eyes. The hospital he'd stayed in the past two days was modern and clean and he was grateful for it. Infection, Jalani had told him, was the most significant threat for burn victims. He'd looked at his back in a mirror and it looked terrible, like burnt wood, but it would heal, and he would live.

"It'll be a reminder that all this was real," Jalani had told him.

She sat in the seat next to him. She hadn't been back to America since her youth, but she was excited and told him all the places she wanted to see: the capital, Mt. Rushmore, the Golden Gate Bridge, the statue of liberty... Eric promised her they could see it all. Once his back stopped feeling like he was lying on a hot frying pan.

He thought back to his interview with the police. He'd met with an inspector for the region. The man didn't write down a single note or record the conversation. He simply smoked a pipe and stared at Eric with un-interested eyes.

"That is quite a story," he finally said. "The hyenas here can get quite large."

Eric realized the man didn't believe him. Or if he did, he didn't care.

Jalani took his hand and leaned back and closed her eyes. They had another ten hours before they landed in New York City. Eric felt the soft euphoria of the pain medication kicking in, and the burning in his back began to subside. He looked at Jalani, her face and hair which fell perfectly over her shoulders, and hoped he would always remember this moment just like this. The moment he knew who he wanted to be with. Will had been right: falling in love was the greatest of all human actions.

He grinned to himself, and then drifted off to sleep.

48

Inspector Patel pulled his car over to the side of the road and got out. The plains spread out before him and the heat seemed unbearable. He had been coming here since he was a child and knew the villagers that lived out here. The last vestige of old India. Of an India that had died out with modernity and would soon vanish altogether. He felt remorse for it. As the plains were developed to cater to the swelling population, the indigenous tribes would die out as well. They were the last link to the ancient people of this land. With them gone, the past would be gone, too.

He went over to the remnants of the burned-out jeep the young American had described to him. Looking around, he saw no carcass of some great beast. There was nothing but trees and tall grass and boulders. Nothing but the landscape. It was possible the American had seen hyenas, and perhaps even large hyenas, but the sizes he had told him were obviously fabricated. He and several of the officers had interviewed him and the woman with him, thinking perhaps he had something to do with the deaths of his friends, but Patel had heard many rumors of the children that disappeared out on the plains and were never seen again. Clans of roaming, man-eating hyenas were a remote possibility, but a possibility nonetheless. Humans were easy prey.

Patel examined the jeep more closely. Anything that had been here of any value was gone, stripped by bandits, villagers, and animals. The jeep itself would rust and become part of the landscape as well, until the villagers, over time, dismantled it and used the metal for weapons for hunting. They were by and large peaceful, but not vegetarian as much of India was. Patel imagined that they ate closely to how their ancestors ate 10,000 years ago.

He knelt down and looked inside the glovebox of the jeep and found a few papers. He flipped through them and then tossed them back. He rose and wiped at the sweat on his brow when he heard it. A rumble.

He thought it was a car at first, something in the distance drawing close. He put his hand over his eyes to block the sunlight but saw nothing. He thought perhaps it was the wind in the trees, but there was little wind, hardly a breeze. Then he heard it again. Closer this time.

Behind him.

He turned and saw the immense mouth. It was higher than he was and he had to look up. The snout split apart to reveal rows of jagged teeth and a large pink tongue. The creature growled. Patel barely got out a single scream, before the mouth clamped down over his head and lifted his body in the air. Tearing head from torso. The sounds of feeding followed. Horrible wet sounds of muscles and sinew being swallowed, bones broken and chewed, and the grunts of a beast that ate skin, bones and teeth as though they were soft meat.

Then, the sounds stopped, and the plains were silent

again.

Made in the USA
Coppell, TX
15 May 2020

25758656R00122